TRAMPLED BLOSSOMS
WHAT THEY STOLE FROM GRANDMA

MOON YOUNG-SOOK

Trampled Blossoms

This is a work of fiction based on true historical facts, in-person interviews, and testimonies of the "comfort women." The names and details of certain real persons, places, and incidents have been changed in the novel, and all other characters, places, and events are products of the author's imagination.

Text copyright © 2016 Moon Young-sook
All rights reserved.

No part of this book may be reproduced in any form without the written permission of the publisher.

Published in 2019 by Seoul Selection U.S.A., Inc.
4199 Campus Drive, Suite 550, Irvine, CA 92612

Phone: 949-509-6584 / Seoul office: 82-2-734-9567
Fax: 949-509-6599 / Seoul office: 82-2-734-9562
E-mail: hankinseoul@gmail.com
Website: www.seoulselection.com

ISBN: 978-1-62412-126-5 51699
Library of Congress Control Number: 2019946644

Printed in the Republic of Korea

TRAMPLED BLOSSOMS
WHAT THEY STOLE FROM GRANDMA

MOON YOUNG-SOOK

Seoul Selection

Contents

7	Grandma Is Missing
20	Mom's Secret
38	A Job at the Textile Mill
63	A Bird with Broken Wings
86	Driven by the Bitter Wind
95	Monsters in My Room
106	Far Across the Sea
117	Our Daily Struggle
134	An Unblessed Baby
155	Run Away with Me
169	Waiting for a Ship
180	My Friend Bok-sun
197	Prisoners of War
208	Mom, I'm Home
231	Keep the Statue Safe
241	A Message from the Author

Grandma Is Missing

Seoul, 2016

It was the day of Yu-ri's middle school graduation. After the graduation ceremony, she'd gone out to eat with her parents. When they opened the front door, they heard the telephone ringing off the hook.

"Who's that? Do you think—?" her mother said, her eyes wide.

Right away, Yu-ri thought of the same person: her grandmother. She was just about the only person who used the landline. They hadn't heard it ring a single time since she'd left the house. Yu-ri dashed over and picked up the receiver.

"Hello? May I ask who is calling?"

Yu-ri heard the voice of a strange woman over the phone. "Ah, hello! Somebody finally picked up! I've been calling since this morning," the woman said. After a pause, she added, "I'm with the House of Sharing."

"The House of Sharing? You must have got the wrong number," Yu-ri said.

But just as she was about to put down the receiver, she heard an urgent voice on the other line. "Hello? I only need a moment!"

Yu-ri put the receiver back against her ear. "Who are you trying to reach? We don't have anything to do with the House of Sharing. I told you you've got the wrong number!"

But then Yu-ri heard something that made her forget all about her irritation.

"Aren't you an acquaintance of Heo Chun-ja? There's something I need to check on."

Yu-ri gasped. "Did you say Chun-ja—Heo Chun-ja?"

Yu-ri's mother, who had followed her into the living room, snatched the receiver away.

"Um, hello," her mother said, "Do you know Heo Chun-ja?"

Heo Chun-ja was the name of Yu-ri's grandmother. Yu-ri's heart was pounding.

"Who's that, honey? Have they found your mother?" Yu-ri's father walked over toward his wife and pressed his ear against the receiver.

Yu-ri's mother switched the receiver to her right hand. "Yes, please go ahead. This is her daughter speaking. Where is she right now?" Yu-ri's mother seemed to be on the verge of running out the door to find her mother.

But then she heard something that left her dumbfounded. "What was that? What did you say?"

Yu-ri's mother reeled. "Yes, of course. Are you really sure? Oh, no. I can't believe this!"

She made an effort to stay calm. "Where are you calling from? Oh, Gwangju? OK. We'll be there right away."

After putting down the receiver, Yu-ri's mother cradled her head in her hands and began to cry.

Yu-ri's father caressed her shoulder. "What's wrong, honey? What happened?"

Yu-ri's mother could barely speak through her sobs. "She's saying that Mom's dead! That can't be true. It just can't be!"

"Try to calm down, honey. They might have got the wrong number, after all. You should have gotten more details before you hung up."

"She definitely said 'Heo Chun-ja.' That's Mom's name. She's apparently at a funeral home just outside of Seoul, in Gwangju. I guess we should go," Mom said, and then paused. "I just don't know what's going on. It doesn't make any sense. There must be some mistake. I can't believe she's dead!"

Yu-ri thought about what had happened three years ago, on the day she'd graduated from elementary school.

Yu-ri had made plans with her friends to go out for pizza and watch a movie that evening. While she was taking photos with her mother and grandmother after the graduation ceremony, her attention had already drifted off to her friends. Yuri's grandmother was holding a bouquet of flowers in one hand and hugging Yu-ri with the other. When the shutter clicked, the old woman's smile stood out like a pink rose in a field of tiny white blossoms of baby's breath.

Yu-ri couldn't wait to say goodbye to her mother and grandmother and go hang out with her friends. Her mother would understand how she felt, but her grandmother wouldn't like the idea. Yu-ri handed her graduation certificate and the rest of her things to her mother and gave her a look, asking for help. Yu-ri's plan was to head toward her classroom and then loop around to where her friends were waiting.

But when she turned to go, her grandmother seemed surprised. "And where are you off to all by yourself?"

Yu-ri's mother took Chun-ja's hand and started moving toward the school entrance, pulling the old woman after her. "Yu-ri said she has some stuff to do with her friends in the classroom. She'll catch up with us."

Chun-ja stared at Yu-ri's mother in dismay. "Are you telling me we're going to go home and leave Yu-ri here alone?"

"Mom, Yu-ri isn't a little girl anymore. She's thirteen years old. So today, I think we should just let her hang out with her friends."

Chun-ja lost her temper. "How can you be so calm about this, being a mother yourself? I'll wait here until Yu-ri's ready to go home, so you just go on ahead."

Yu-ri's breath caught in her throat. She'd been hoping to sneak off without her grandmother noticing.

Yu-ri let out a sigh. "Grandma, why don't you go home with Mom? I'll be there right away."

The old woman shook her head. "Yu-ri, you're thirteen years old now. You can't go running around by yourself! You just do whatever you want, and I'll tag along without getting in the way."

Yu-ri was even more angry that her grandmother assumed she wouldn't be in the way.

"Grandma, I'm not going to be by myself. I'm going to be with my friends! Can you please just go home with Mom?"

Yu-ri's friends had gotten tired of waiting and walked over toward them.

"Hey, Yu-ri! What are you waiting for? We're hungry. Let's get going!" said a boy in Yu-ri's class, grabbing her by the arm.

Yu-ri's grandmother smacked the boy on the arm with her wrinkled hand.

"Get your hand off her! Did someone give you permission to touch her? Let go of her right now!"

Yu-ri's friends stared at her grandmother in shock.

"Hey, that hurts! I'm Yu-ri's friend, you know," the boy said before turning back toward Yu-ri. "When are you ever going to stop being the glass princess?"

Yu-ri held back a sob. Some of the nastier boys at school had dubbed her the "glass princess." The joke was that Yu-ri (which happens to be the Korean word for glass) would shatter like glass if her grandmother weren't around to look after her. She really hated that nickname.

Yu-ri snapped. "Grandma, please just leave me alone! Stop following me around all the time."

Yu-ri yelled to her friends. "Let's get out of here!"

The kids sprinted out of the school gate as if they were doing a 100-meter dash. Yu-ri's grandmother hobbled along behind them, calling Yu-ri's name. But given her advanced age and faltering step, she could hardly hope to catch up with the preteens, who were loping along like gazelles. She gradually fell farther and farther behind.

Yu-ri didn't want to look behind her. She cared much less about her grandmother than about getting respect from her friends. Her grandmother was like a glob of gum stuck to her shoe that just wouldn't come off, no matter how hard she tugged at it. She wanted to keep running until her grandmother was out of sight.

Ever since Yu-ri was a little girl, her grandmother hadn't let her go outside by herself. When Yu-ri went to lessons after school, her grandmother would hang around outside, and when school got out late, her grandmother would be outside the gate, waiting fretfully for her. Yu-ri's group activities sometimes required her to leave school with boys from her class, and time after time her grandmother had seized her hand and marched her home, as if her classmates had been creepy old men. When the two of them were walking down the street one day, a male stranger had brushed past Yu-ri. This had startled her grandmother so much she threw her arms around Yu-ri and didn't let go until the man was far down the street.

Yu-ri and her friends were having a great time as they chatted and nibbled on the pizza, spicy *tteokbokki* rice cakes, and *gimbap* rolls they'd ordered. Yu-ri felt so relieved not to have her grandmother there beside her. When the group walked into the movie theater, Yu-ri felt as if she were entering a strange new world, a world beyond her grandmother's reach.

But when Yu-ri and her friends walked outside after the movie, her grandmother was there outside the exit, frantically looking in all directions. All the strength drained from Yu-ri's legs. As soon as her grandmother saw Yu-ri, the old woman hurried over and threw her arms around her granddaughter.

"Yu-ri, my baby girl! I was so worried about you!"

As Yu-ri's friends slipped away from her, she heard them laughing. One of them said, "I guess Yu-ri will be the glass princess forever!" Yu-ri was fuming, but she couldn't let her friends see her griping to her grandmother.

Meanwhile, Yu-ri's grandmother had taken hold of Yu-ri's hand and squeezed tightly, as if she would never let go. "Did you get something to eat, sweetie?"

When Yu-ri didn't answer, her grandmother went on. "You've gone and grown up on me! I do believe you're starting to look like a young woman. All the more reason to look after yourself!"

Yu-ri remained silent. "Why aren't you answering me?" her grandmother asked.

The whole way home, Yu-ri didn't say a word, as if her lips were glued together. Her grandmother's attention just made her feel trapped and suffocated.

As soon as they got home, Yu-ri unloaded her frustration on her mother.

"Mom, I think I'm going crazy! It stresses me out just to see Grandma. I can't stand it."

Yu-ri was so upset that her face was red and her hands were shaking.

"Today must have been really hard on you, Yu-ri," her mother said. Her grandmother vanished into her room, tut-tutting.

"Oh, I'm just so sick of her!" Yu-ri whined. Her mother gave her a warning look.

"Mom, didn't you say things weren't easy for you, either? Can you tell Grandma to give me a little space now? My friends look at me like a freak! You know what they said to me? They said I must've been sexually abused when I was little. They said that's probably why Grandma is so overprotective. It's so embarrassing!"

At that moment, Yu-ri's grandmother came out of her room and scolded Yu-ri. "Which one of those boys said that to you? He's really going to get it! Yu-ri, I'm doing this all for your sake. You don't understand how rough it is out there."

Yu-ri had run out of patience. "Grandma, didn't you see my friends teasing me about being a 'glass princess'? I'm so sick of you! I can barely breathe when you're around."

Yu-ri's mother raised her eyebrows. "Young lady, I won't let you speak to your grandmother like that."

"You told me you used to get fed up about how overbearing she was, too!"

"Yeah, I did. I know how you feel, Yu-ri, but—"

"If you really know how I feel, then make her give me a

little space! She is literally suffocating me."

Yu-ri's mother sighed. "I had a really hard time, too, Mom. Don't you think Yu-ri has her reasons for acting like this?"

Yu-ri's grandmother shook her head. "I was a devoted mother to you, and Yu-ri deserves to be raised the same way."

Now it was Yu-ri's mother who was shaking her head, and an edge came into her voice.

"Mom, it's great to be devoted to your kids, but what Yu-ri is saying is she feels suffocated. I barely managed to put up with you because you're my mother, but you're Yu-ri's grandmother. Besides, thirteen-year-olds are pretty much grown-ups these days. I can't stand to see Yu-ri going through such a hard time."

This speech seemed to have an effect. Yu-ri's grandmother muttered to herself and sighed several times in a row. Yu-ri fervently hoped that her grandmother would own up to her extreme paranoia.

After a long pause, the old woman spoke. "Neither of you get it, do you? I guess there's no way you could get it."

Pain was written all over her face. After another long sigh, she went on in a low voice, as if she were talking to herself.

"I wish I weren't like this either, but I can't help it. Sometimes, I think I'm taking things too far, but when I have one of those awful dreams I just feel so anxious."

Yu-ri's mother tried to comfort the old woman. "Mom, you've always told me you can't control yourself. That's why I think you should see a doctor sometime."

Yu-ri's grandmother let out another sigh, this one even heavier than before.

"I'm not going to see a doctor. It wouldn't help if I did. God knows I've lived a full life. It's time for me to pass on. There's no point wasting any more time in this painful world."

Tears welled up in the old woman's eyes and rolled down her cheeks. Yu-ri's mother handed her a tissue.

"Mom, what's this about dying? All I'm asking you to do is cut Yu-ri a little slack! You know, I'm getting sick of this, too."

Yu-ri slipped away to her room. Her mother and grandmother's voices were gradually getting louder.

"Mom, you've never been normal! You know how paranoid you were about me. I felt suffocated, too! I'm sure it was hard for you as well. So please go see a doctor and get some help!"

"No, I won't do that. There's no need to."

"Why won't you even consider it? I'm really fed up with you, Mom. Sometimes you run off and wander the streets late at night. When it's freezing outside in the wintertime, you go and open up the windows because you're burning up inside while the rest of us sit there shivering. And now even Yu-ri is having a tough time. You need to let the doctors figure out what it is that caused your condition."

"I know what's wrong with me. It's not the sort of thing a doctor can cure. It's no big deal."

"No big deal? Don't you know how hard it was for Dad, too? I'm telling you, you need to get tested so we can figure out the cause and get you some treatment!"

Even in her room, Yu-ri could hear her mother's voice ringing.

"And I'm telling you, it's not that kind of disease!" Yu-ri's grandmother said, matching her daughter's volume.

"Don't give me that crap! Even Yu-ri says you're driving her crazy!"

Yu-ri put her head down on her desk and covered her ears. Part of her wished that her grandmother would just vanish into thin air.

And early the next morning, Chun-ja vanished. For the first few days, the family thought she would be back any day. But a week, ten days, and then a month passed by without any sign of her. Not only that, but the old woman had covered her tracks. Yu-ri's mother filed a missing person report at the police station and went around looking for her. She visited several hospitals in case the old woman had gotten in an accident, but she didn't turn up anything. Yu-ri herself was always troubled by the thought that her grandmother had left the family because of her.

Then exactly three years later, on the day that Yu-ri graduated from middle school, the family got word that her grandmother had died.

Mom's Secret

House of Sharing, 2016

Yu-ri followed her parents to the front door and watched them rush off.

What on earth could have happened to Grandma?

As Yu-ri wandered around the living room, her eyes were suddenly drawn to a photo in the cabinet. It was the photo she'd taken with her grandmother on the day of her elementary school graduation. In the photo, Yu-ri's grandmother seemed to be staring out at her with a big grin. Yu-ri couldn't meet her grandmother's eyes. The thought that she'd never get to see her grandmother again brought a rush of guilt. If only she hadn't been so nasty to her grandmother that day, Yu-ri thought, the old woman might not have left the house. Yu-ri quickly put the frame back, facedown, to hide the photo.

It was past 10 o'clock when Yu-ri finally got a call from

her mother.

"Yu-ri, you're going to have to stay by yourself tonight."

"Home alone? That's scary! Are you sure it's Grandma? Is she really dead?"

"Yeah, I'm sure," Mom said, and let out a sob.

The crying gradually grew louder on the other end of the phone. Since her mother didn't seem able to continue the conversation, Yu-ri was left with little choice.

"OK, I can take care of myself."

"We'll drop by briefly early in the morning. Make sure you lock the door before going to bed. If you feel scared, leave the lights on."

As soon as she'd hung up the phone, Yu-ri turned the lights on in every room. She had a weird feeling that her grandmother was watching from somewhere. Yu-ri turned on the television, too, and then cranked up the volume. She didn't sleep very well that night, repeatedly dozing off only to return to a half-conscious state.

The next morning, Yu-ri was jerked from her sleep by the front door. It was 6 o'clock, and her parents were home. Her mother's eyes were red and puffy.

"Mom, is Grandma actually dead?"

"She is, Yu-ri. She's gone," her mother said, still crying.

"Where was she all that time?"

"I don't know what's going on. How could this have happened? I mean, how is this even possible?"

Yu-ri's mother couldn't go on, so her father filled her in.

"We're here to get a change of clothes. We have to hurry back to the funeral home."

"Can I go, too?"

Yu-ri's mother, who was putting on a different outfit, shook her head.

"Honey," her father said cautiously, "Don't you think we should take Yu-ri with us? It would give her a chance to say goodbye to her grandmother."

"She can't go."

Yu-ri was hurt by this blunt refusal. She had the feeling that her mother blamed her for her grandmother leaving the house and dying away from her family.

"Why not? Why can't I go?"

Before Yu-ri could even finish, her mother cut in.

"The fact is that you don't need to go. Why don't you just send up a prayer for Grandma to end up in a better place."

The words seemed to pierce Yu-ri's heart. "Mom, I feel bad about a lot of the things I did to Grandma. Please let me have a chance to say goodbye."

"I told you to let it drop, so just let it drop. I have my reasons."

Yu-ri's father interjected. "Honey, we need to get moving!"

As soon as Yu-ri's parents finished changing, they were out the door, without even sitting down.

Yu-ri couldn't figure her mother out.

Why is she so determined not to bring me with them? She said she has her reasons, but what could they be? Where was Grandma that whole time?

Yu-ri took the photograph out of the cabinet and stared intently at her grandmother.

Yu-ri wanted to ask her grandmother for forgiveness and wished she could go to the funeral home, even if that meant going alone. She suddenly remembered that the woman who'd called yesterday had said she was from the House of Sharing.

I wonder where the House of Sharing is.

Yu-ri got on the Internet to search for the House of Sharing. She found a number of locations by that name: retirement communities, nursing homes, and residential facilities for people with disabilities. There was another one, too: a home for some of the former comfort women. But Yu-ri's grandmother didn't have anything to do with the comfort women.

Maybe it's a nursing home?

Yu-ri searched for nursing homes called the House of Sharing. Her mom had definitely mentioned the city of Gwangju, but there were no funeral homes in Gwangju by that name.

When Yu-ri's parents returned home the next evening, they were completely wiped out. As soon as her mother went into her room, she flopped down onto the bed. Her voice was hoarse, and there were dark circles under her eyes. Yu-ri's father walked around the house on tiptoe so as not to disturb her.

Yu-ri learned that her grandmother's body had been cremated and the ashes scattered around the town where she'd grown up.

I guess she liked the idea of going home better than being laid to rest next to Grandpa.

Yu-ri had never been to that town herself, but she'd heard about it from her grandmother.

For a few days after the funeral, a peculiar mood settled over Yu-ri's home, and her mother and father seemed to have their lips taped shut. Yu-ri knew how painful this all must be for her mother, who had looked for her own mother so long only to lose her like this. So out of respect for her mother, Yu-ri made up her mind to keep her questions on the back burner until her mother could cope with her sadness.

There was so much that Yu-ri wanted to know about her grandmother. Her father seemed to be avoiding eye contact with her as well. Even so, he was easier to approach than her mother, who wouldn't even let her broach the topic. Yu-ri thought her father might give something away if she asked him about it.

After dinner one night, Yu-ri's mother headed straight to her room. Yu-ri thought this was her chance.

"Dad, who was that woman who called our house?"

"It was someone at the place where your grandma spent her final years."

"How did they get our phone number?"

Yu-ri's father hesitated for a moment. That very moment, her mother flung open the door to her room and called to her father. Yu-ri felt as if she'd been caught talking about some big secret.

"I want you to wait out here, Yu-ri. There's something I need to discuss with your father," Yu-ri's mother said. She seemed distracted, as if something was bothering her.

Seeing her mother so agitated made Yu-ri's curiosity snowball.

She's hiding something from me. What is it that she doesn't want me to hear?

Yu-ri got close to the door and pressed her ear against it. Her mother's voice came very faintly to her ear.

"Honey, I don't want you to tell Yu-ri anything about this."

Yu-ri could hear her father a little more clearly.

"Honey, I don't understand why you didn't let Yu-ri go to the funeral. Yu-ri's not a little girl now; she's about to start high school. I know you were shocked by what happened to your mother, but you suddenly seem like a different person. Nothing has changed about our family; it's the same now as it always has been. So I hope you'll go back to normal soon. You need to tell Yu-ri the truth, too."

Yu-ri could hear her mother weeping. None of their conversation made any sense to her.

What did Dad mean when he said that nothing has changed about our family? What is it that I'm not supposed to know? Is Mom not my real mother?

Yu-ri suddenly felt as if she were all alone. Crazy ideas whizzed around her head. She couldn't hold it in any longer.

"Open up the door, Mom! Why are you leaving me out of this?"

The conversation inside the room suddenly cut off, but the door stayed shut. For a moment, Yu-ri felt an awful foreboding. She was sure there was some secret she wasn't supposed to know. She angrily banged on the door. After some time, the door opened. Her mother was standing there, with tears in her eyes.

"Mom, I've got to know the reason! What's going on? What's the secret I'm not supposed to know about?" That all came out more harshly than she'd intended.

"I'm sorry, Yu-ri. I'll tell you everything when the time is right. But for right now, I need you to just pretend that nothing happened. Can you do that for me?"

"No, Mom, you need to tell me right now. It was weird how overprotective Grandma used to be. She sheltered me as if she thought someone was going to snatch me away. As long as she was living with us, she never took her eyes off me. I'm really upset that she passed away, too. While you and Dad were gone, I did a lot of thinking about the past and the mistakes I've made. But it's been really weird in the house since Grandma died. You won't tell me anything and seem to be hiding something. What's going on with you? Why are you leaving me out of this? What is it that you're not telling me? Are you not really my Mom? Did Grandma bring me to the family? Are you nervous that I'm going to figure out your secret? Is that why you didn't let me go to the funeral?"

Everything that Yu-ri had been imagining over the past few days came pouring out, as if a dam had burst.

Her mother's face turned pale, and she shook her head vehemently. "That's not what this is about, Yu-ri. This is between your grandma and me. It has nothing to do with you. I see your imagination has been running wild. This isn't your problem, Yu-ri. It's mine. The thing is, it's just so hard for me to deal with. Can you please hang on just a little longer? I'm begging you, Yu-ri."

Yu-ri's mother began to weep, as she held her face in her hands.

That was when Yu-ri's father spoke up. "Honey, I can't imagine how frustrated Yu-ri must have been to imagine all that. None of this is your fault or your mother's fault, either. No matter how hard this is for you, it doesn't compare to what your mother went through. It's all the fault of our country's tragic history. That's why we should be honest with Yu-ri—"

With a start, Yu-ri's mother interrupted him. "Honey, I can't do that yet. I'll tell her later myself."

In embarrassment, Yu-ri's father spoke to his daughter in a gentle voice. "At any rate, Yu-ri, this has nothing to do with you. This is about your mom and grandma, so don't let your imagination get carried away, OK?"

Since Yu-ri's mother refused to open up, the cave of secrets seemed to be growing deeper and deeper.

"By the way, honey," Yu-ri's father said, "What happened at the House of Sharing today? Did you figure anything out?"

The House of Sharing was exactly what Yu-ri had been wondering about. "Dad, you're not talking about the place where the old comfort women live, are you?"

But her mother interjected before her father could answer. "We don't know all the details yet. I'll tell you about that later."

Her mother's evasive answer made Yu-ri feel certain that her parents were talking about the place the comfort women lived.

Why would Grandma have died at a home for comfort women, of all places?

After Yu-ri's mother returned from her visit to the House of Sharing, she began leaving the house early in the morning and not coming home until late in the evening. Yu-ri was feeling more and more sure that her grandmother was somehow connected to the House of Sharing. Out of the blue, Yu-ri's mother had started cooking food to take to the House of Sharing. Then a few days later, she helped bathe the women living at the home, which left her so tired that she collapsed on the couch as soon as she got home.

"Mom, was Grandma connected in some way to the House of Sharing?"

"She was in a big way, Yu-ri. I'm going to tell you all about it later. But right now, I'm so tired. I need to get some rest."

Yu-ri's mother disappeared into her room, apparently not in the mood to answer any more questions.

I guess I'll have to figure this out myself.

Yu-ri's mother had always watched soap operas and taken little interest in social issues or politics. But after Grandma Chun-ja's death, her mother started focusing on Korea and Japan's troubled past. Yu-ri found it really bizarre how much attention her mother paid to the comfort women agreement signed by the South Korean and Japanese governments soon after her grandmother's death.

Yu-ri got online to look up the House of Sharing in Gwangju and figure out how to get there. Though her grandmother couldn't have been a comfort woman, Yu-ri wanted to visit the place her grandmother had spent her final days, especially since Yu-ri hadn't gotten to attend the funeral. After all, her grandmother had cherished Yu-ri and taken good care of her. As the only grandchild, Yu-ri felt she owed her that much.

Days flew by, and before Yu-ri knew it, half of her vacation was over and high school was approaching. On Sunday morning, her mother headed out to attend a rally. She was joining other protesters who wanted the government to annul its comfort women agreement with Japan. As it happened, Yu-ri's father was out of town on business, leaving Yu-ri home alone. So she grabbed the directions to the House of Sharing that she'd printed out and left the house.

It took quite a while to reach the House of Sharing. Yu-ri had to make two transfers on the subway, get on a bus, and take a taxi. If her grandmother had been alive and aware that Yu-ri had gone off on her own like that, she'd probably have been as fearful as if an earthquake had struck and a tsunami was on its way. On her way to the House of Sharing, Yu-ri kept wondering why her grandmother had gone there and what it had been like to live there. But she couldn't think of anything that would link her grandmother to the comfort women.

There were gentle hills rising behind the House of Sharing and a few plots of farmland in front of it. In front of the entrance to the facility was a cluster of teenage girls in school uniforms. Yu-ri went over and joined the group of girls. An older woman, apparently a tour guide, came over and greeted the girls. The woman told them that they'd start by looking around the history museum and then be given their assignments. Yu-ri guessed the girls were there to do some volunteer work.

The House of Sharing consisted of two buildings, a history museum and the residence where the former comfort women lived. A small garden between the two buildings contained some tall pine trees and, beside them, bronze busts of former comfort women who had passed away. Filled with a sudden curiosity, Yu-ri took a closer look at the sculptures, but her grandmother wasn't among them.

I guess I let my imagination get carried away.

Yu-ri followed the students into the history museum. The items on display there illustrated the horrors endured by the innocent young girls who'd been forced to work for the Japanese army. There were black-and-white photographs, documents from the comfort stations that had been set up at every Japanese military base, and pictures painted by the comfort women themselves.

As Yu-ri looked around the museum, she kept wondering what her grandmother's connection was to the comfort women. She still couldn't puzzle it out.

Why did Grandma spend her last days here?

Yu-ri was too nervous to pay much attention to what the tour guide was saying, and she kept checking the time. The girls who were volunteering took pictures, jotted down notes, and asked questions, which made the tour last much longer than Yu-ri had expected.

When the tour guide and the girls left the museum, Yu-ri followed them out and into the residence of the women. Although the women here had once been comfort women, there didn't seem anything special about them. They looked pretty much the same as any other elderly women.

Yu-ri slipped away from the group and headed to the office. When she opened the door and stepped inside, a female employee looked up at her.

"Is something the matter? You're one of the students who

are here for volunteer work, right?"

Yu-ri shook her head.

"Oh, so you came here by yourself? We have been getting some students lately who come on their own for their homework assignments. Is there something I can help you with?" The woman cocked her head, expectantly.

"Actually, I'm here about Heo Chun-ja," Yu-ri began, but as soon as she got to the name, the woman started and leaped from her chair.

"Heo Chun-ja? She passed away not long ago. Is she an acquaintance of yours?"

"Yes, she's my maternal grandmother."

"My goodness! So were you the girl in that photograph with the phone number on it? The graduation photo where Ms. Heo was holding the bouquet? Come to think of it, you *are* the girl in the photo! That photo is what put us in touch with Ms. Heo's daughter. It's great to meet you! But your mother didn't come today, so what brings you here on your own?"

"My mother doesn't know I'm here. But what's this photo you're talking about?"

Yu-ri was fascinated that the woman had recognized her. Just then, there was a commotion outside the office. The woman asked Yu-ri to wait for a moment and stepped outside. Yu-ri's heart was pounding. She had a feeling that her curiosity was about to be satisfied. The woman swept back in, carrying a heavy box of books.

"You came at the perfect time! Ms. Heo's oral history has just come out."

"Her oral history? What do you mean?" Yu-ri felt bewildered.

The woman looked up as a middle-aged man stepped into the office. "The oral history book has just come in, sir."

From the woman's respectful tone of voice, Yu-ri guessed this man was the director of the House of Sharing.

"Is that right? And who might this young lady be?"

"She says she's the granddaughter of Heo Chun-ja. She's the girl in the photo."

"This is the girl in the photo?" The director opened a desk drawer and removed a photograph—the same one that was framed in Yu-ri's living room.

"Wait a second! How did this picture get here?"

"Didn't you know? Your grandmother always carried this around with her. The phone number on the back is how we were able to get in touch with your mother. Hasn't she told you about that yet?"

The director handed Yu-ri the photograph. Her grandmother's touch was obvious: it was lined with creases, and the corners were worn. On the back of the photo was Yu-ri's home phone number, written in her grandmother's hand.

"I'm really confused about all this. Did my grandma live here?"

"She sure did. You're in luck, actually, since the oral history book just came out. It's a shame the book didn't come out a little sooner. Just ten days earlier, and your grandmother could have seen it."

The director pulled a copy out of the box. "You'll want to take one of these with you and read it. It tells the story of the other comfort women, too."

Yu-ri felt a pang in her chest, as if she'd gulped down a smoothie too fast.

An oral history book for the comfort women? If Grandma's story is in there, wouldn't that mean she was a comfort woman?

"So was my grandma a comfort woman? Is that why she was living here?" Yu-ri asked hesitantly.

The director nodded, pursing his lips. "Your mother was also shocked to learn the whole truth. Hadn't you heard anything about your mother and grandmother's story?"

"Nothing at all. In fact, the reason I'm here is to find out what's going on with my mom. She's been acting so weird since my grandma died."

"I see. Your mother wouldn't have found it easy to talk about that."

"I had no idea my grandma was a comfort woman. To be

honest, I'm still having trouble believing it."

"Your mother probably meant to tell you about it after she'd come to terms with it herself. After all, it takes a while to wrap your head around something like this. Even so, I've been touched by your mother's devotion to the women at the House of Sharing. She also told us she plans to attend the Wednesday demonstrations in the future."

The director paused for a moment. "Yu-ri, reading the oral history book is going to be really painful."

Yu-ri had thought that getting some answers would be a big relief, but instead it felt like a big rock was pressing down on her chest.

"If you want to know how much your grandmother cared about you, why she decided to run away, and why she spent her final years here, it's all in this book. You'll probably learn more about her story from this book than if you'd heard it from your mother."

The director flipped open the book and held it out to Yu-ri. "This is the part where your grandmother's story starts."

Yu-ri's hands trembled as she took the book. "Sir, please don't tell my mother I was here. I'll tell her myself after I've finished the book."

"OK, I won't tell her."

Yu-ri said goodbye to the director and left the office. The book was called *Koreans Kidnapped and Forced to Be Com-*

fort Women for the Japanese Army. It told the stories of five former comfort women. Yu-ri couldn't wait to read it.

When Yu-ri got home, there was no one there. This was the first time she'd been happy to come home to an empty house. Yu-ri locked the door of her room. Taking a deep breath, she opened the book.

A Job at the Textile Mill

Seosan, Chungcheong Province, 1937

The slopes of Mt. Dobisan were draped with a pink blanket of azalea flowers, and I was on my way home from the market. I'd just sold some oysters that I'd dug up over on Ganwoldo Island.

That island had long been famed for its oysters, which had apparently even been served at the royal palace. From the winter until the early spring—when the oysters were swollen with eggs—the villagers of Hakdoljae would go out to the mudbanks to dig up oysters for the market.

When the worst of winter was over and the azaleas began to bloom, the ocean waters grew warm. That was when the oysters began to spawn, secreting their firm white eggs. I'd been poking around for oysters until the tide came in, but didn't find nearly as many as I had in the winter.

On top of that, the oysters were selling for much less

than they had on previous market days. I didn't earn much from the sale, but just holding the bills in my hand got me itching to buy something. The whole time I was in the market, my eyes were drawn to things I wanted to buy: a hand mirror and a pink hair ribbon embroidered with peonies. I had to content myself with some window shopping, fingering the wad of bills in my pocket, before reluctantly turning to go.

When I reached a fork in the road, which led toward Taean in one direction and toward Buseok in the other, I saw a truck rumbling up from Taean, kicking up a white cloud of dust and dirt. In a seaside village such as mine, where the only vehicles were oxcarts, a truck barreling down the road was sure to grab the attention of both young and old.

Most of the people in Hakdoljae had never ridden in a car. Downtown in Seosan, there was a bus that could take you to the big city. But for the most part, the villagers had no reason to leave town, and most of them never did. When people working in the fields heard a honk, they would stand up and stretch their backs as they watched the car drive by. Only when it had vanished into a black dot in the distance would they squat back down to their work.

The truck racing down the road screeched to a stop right in front of me. The cloud of dust reeked of gasoline. The door of the truck opened, letting out a policeman from the Hakdoljae station and a Japanese man, his hair gleaming with pomade.

My heart sank, and I unconsciously took a step backward. For Koreans, the police were more frightening than any tiger. People joked that even a hungry baby would stop bawling if you said a policeman was on his way.

The policeman walked straight over to me. "Aren't you the girl from the family in that ravine in Hakdoljae?"

A horrible glint came into the policeman's eye when he recognized me.

"You *are* that girl! There's no fooling these eyes of mine. I got a good look at you at your dad's funeral last summer. It's a good thing I ran into you, since I was on my way to your house anyway."

The policeman had been snooping around my house ever since my dad came back from Manchuria. There was something unnerving about the peculiar gleam of his eyes. They reminded me of a cat's eyes, shifting with the light.

With an obsequious bow to the Japanese man, the policeman gestured to me. "What do you think, sir? A bit young, but she's quite comely, isn't she?"

The Japanese man looked me up and down with a smirk. "How would you like to make some money? There's a lot to be made if you work at a textile mill in Japan. All you have to do is come with me."

My ears perked up at the word "money," and I thought of my mom. As our debt kept piling up, she would stay hunched over late into the night doing needlework she took on for extra money. After we racked up debt buying medication for my sick dad, the old man who ran the pharmacy started paying frequent visits to my mother to bully her over the debt, asking when she intended to pay up. The villagers whispered that the lecherous old pharmacist actually had something else in mind and was using the debt as an excuse to visit so often.

Just a few days ago, the old pharmacist had dropped by once again, late in the evening. After taking a seat on our front porch, he'd begun haranguing my mom. "Starting next month, you're going to have to start paying off the principal on top of the interest. It's only out of the kindness of my heart that I've held off on the principal until now. If you can't pay, I'll have to take that daughter of yours and put her to work. I'm not running some kind of charity here."

Just thinking about that scene made my skin crawl. There were even rumors that the old pharmacist had a habit of taking little kids as his concubines.

Working at a textile mill in Japan might be better than going to that old man's house. It's hard enough to keep up with the interest. How are we supposed to pay back the principal, too?

When I hesitated, the policeman urged me to make up my mind. "From what I hear, your family is in debt to that pharmacy in town. If you get a job at the textile mill in Japan, you can earn money and pay off that debt, too. All the women in town are lined up to go, but I was coming out here to give you first dibs. What luck that I happened to run into you like this!"

The old pharmacist's regular visits had apparently clued the townspeople in to our debt. If there was really some way to make money, I was willing to do just about anything. Hearing that the women in town were lined up to go made me antsy.

"When would I have to go, Officer?"

"You've got to go right now. If you're going, get in the truck!"

"Let me ask my mother first."

"There's no time for that," the Japanese man interjected. "In a month, you can send your wages to your family. I bet your mom will like getting that money. In Japan, a month's pay is a ton of money—enough to buy a whole bag of rice. We need to get a move on."

I found myself picturing how delighted my mom would be to get that money a month from now.

If I go to Japan, maybe I can find Jin-gyu, too!

Jin-gyu, Mr. Yun's second son, had always looked after me as if I'd been his little sister. Seeing him striding to the town's high school in his student's cap and uniform had made me feel as exhilarated as a skylark hopping along the edge of the barley field. A year had already passed since Jin-gyu had gone to Japan. Thinking of him made my earlobes tingle.

"But I still need to go home and say goodbye to my mom and pack my clothes and other stuff."

"No, we're out of time. Hurry up and get in the truck." The policeman picked me up bodily and put me inside.

"Stop it! My mom—"

The truck began moving forward, belching out black smoke. I didn't want to leave without telling my mom goodbye.

"Let me out! I've got something to give my mom, and also—"

"You don't need to worry about it," the policeman said, interrupting me. "When I see your mom, I'll tell her all about it. Anyway, she'll be happy to hear you've gone off to make some money."

It was so noisy in the truck I could barely hear what the policeman was saying. The truck was going too fast for me to jump out, either.

As the truck headed toward town, I held out the wad of bills to the policeman. "Can you give this money to my mom for me? I got it from selling oysters. I'd really appreciate it if you could do that for me."

I quietly bade a sad farewell to Mt. Dobisan, which was fading into the distance behind us. While I was afraid of leaving my mom, I also felt a little relieved. I wouldn't have to poke around for oysters to sell at the market or lug around jugs of water or firewood anymore.

Once I get my monthly wages, I'll send them all to my mom!

The thought that I could help my mom out soothed my nerves. Once I'd earned some money, the first thing I would do was pay off our debt to the old pharmacist in town. After that, I'd buy a pretty indigo silk skirt for my mother, who was so busy doing other people's sewing she didn't have time for her own. I also wanted to buy some neat-looking sneakers for my little brother Chun-sik, who had nothing to wear but some torn-up black rubber shoes.

The truck kept going, and before long we passed the marketplace in town. When the truck pulled up in front of the police station, the policeman hopped out.

"Make sure to tell my mom about everything. Don't forget to give her that money, too!"

The policeman waved his hand reassuringly. Now it was

just me and the Japanese man in the truck. Being alone with him made me nervous. Leaving Seosan, the truck was heading into unfamiliar territory, places I'd never been before. My longtime dream of riding in a car had finally come true, but rather than feeling excited, my head was crowded with all kinds of concerns.

Can I make it safely to Japan? Is there really a job waiting for me there? How am I going to feed myself? What kind of work will I do at the textile mill? Where am I going to sleep?

These questions kept rattling around my head as the truck rattled down the road.

The truck stopped at a fork in the road, in front of a tavern. A man helped two women into the truck. The women, both strangers, looked older than me, but I was glad not to be by myself with the Japanese man anymore.

"Just a minute, now. We need to talk to our moms first!"

I guessed these women hadn't had a chance to say goodbye to their families, either.

"Cut the crap, will you? I've already promised to get you a job and enough rice to fill your belly," the Japanese man growled, glaring at the women. His tone of voice was gruff now, far different than when he'd first spoken to me.

When the sun started sinking into the west, we reached a train track. Someone said we were in the town of Gwangcheon, a major producer of pickled shrimp. I'd heard that the train ran through Gwangcheon, but this was my first time to actually see it. It was amazing to see the pitch-black train roll by, puffing out white smoke. The truck followed a road that ran alongside the railroad tracks. I was starting to feel dizzy and nauseated and thought I might throw up.

The red glow of the sunset in the west had faded into a deep purple by the time the truck stopped in front of an inn near Daecheon Station. As soon as I got out of the truck, I squatted down on the roadside and retched for a while. The nausea, I learned, was carsickness. I wasn't the only one, though. The two other women were just as carsick as I was.

A handful of other women were already waiting in our room at the inn. They said they were on their way to Japan, just like me. Sitting in twos and threes with people from the same village, the women looked at us nervously. The innkeeper, a woman, came round and handed us rice balls for dinner, but I felt far too queasy to eat anything. Even when I lay down, the ceiling kept spinning above my head.

I felt like I'd barely closed my eyes when the sound of muffled voices woke me up—it was the next morning already. The innkeeper came by with some more rice balls. Since I'd skipped dinner, I scarfed down the chewy ball of salted rice and barley in a single bite.

Before long, I heard a car pull up and loud jabbering outside. The innkeeper told us to get our stuff together and come out. When I stepped outside the inn, the Japanese man who'd brought us there was waiting in the truck. We all got back in the truck and continued down the unfamiliar road. Each time the truck stopped, different men would bring women over and put them in the truck. The women all looked as nervous as cattle on their way to market. My bottom got awfully sore as the truck bounced along the rocky and bumpy country road. If there had been a roof on the truck, I'd probably have gotten a bump on my head, too.

The truck stopped just before sunset at a point on the coast that someone said was near the port of Samcheonpo. The Japanese man took us to an inn where the rooms were full of women, eighteen altogether. All the women at the inn were on their way to a new job, just like me. I seemed to be the youngest of the bunch.

The Japanese man was talking to the man who ran the inn. "Keep an eye on them to make sure none of them run off."

"You can count on me, sir," the innkeeper said in an ingratiating tone, even though he looked much older. The Japanese man got back in the truck and drove off.

It's not like we're convicts, so why does someone need to watch us and make sure we don't run off?

I'd spent two grueling days in that truck, and as soon as I reached my room I fell asleep right away. The next day, the women weren't allowed to leave their rooms. The only thing we had to eat was rice balls twice a day, and when we needed to use the bathroom, we had to be quick about it because the innkeeper was watching. I didn't understand why the Japanese man was worried about us running away when he'd brought us here to give us jobs.

In an attempt to calm my nerves, I pictured myself working at the textile mill in Japan.

What kind of work uniform will I have? I suppose everyone will wear the same uniform to work. I wonder what my job will be at a factory full of machines. Whatever the job is, I've got to diligently learn my duties so I can earn a lot of money, too.

Imagining this kind of thing made the wait a little less tedious.

Once again, we had rice balls for dinner. The main ingredient this time was barley, sprinkled with rice. There was so little rice that I could count the grains.

"So much for white rice with meat on the side," muttered the woman next to me as she nibbled on her rice ball.

"What kind of work will we do at the textile mill? You don't think it'll be too difficult, do you?"

"I'll be happy with any kind of job. There are a ton of factories in Japan."

The women in the room were all excited at the prospect

of making money, and I quietly listened to their chatter.

"They told me I'm going to a silk weaving factory. They say it's a new factory, so they need a lot of people."

"I guess they're planning to take a bunch of people all at once. Oh, I can't wait to go!"

"I need to hurry up and make some money so I can pay off my debt."

The woman next to me eyed me more closely. "You look so young! What's your age?"

"I'm thirteen."

"What? Thirteen? So they even have jobs for kids like you?"

"That's right. They promised to set me up at a textile mill."

Another woman spoke up. "They must really be short of workers if they're taking kids so young. Anyhow, I wonder when we're going to leave."

Hearing all this made me feel a little grateful to the Japanese man for bringing along someone as young as me.

Whenever we heard the rattle of the truck, everyone would rush to pack their things and get ready to go. But every time, the Japanese man would bring more women to the inn and then vanish.

After a few days of this, one of the women began weeping.

"My mom must wonder where I am. If I knew we'd have to wait like this, I would've told her I was leaving."

"Same here! I bet it's a real mess back at home."

"My mom didn't want me to come so I had to sneak out of the house. I bet she's looking all over for me right now!"

My family was on my mind, too.

Mom and Chun-sik must be so worried about me! I wonder if that policeman actually gave Mom the money I made at the market.

As the wait dragged on and on, my anxiety began to creep back in.

They said there wasn't enough time to visit Mom, as if we were about to depart for Japan. I don't get what the big hurry was if they were just going to drop us off at this inn like a bunch of luggage.

If only the innkeeper hadn't been keeping an eye on us, I would have made a quick trip back home to tell my mom the whole story.

I found myself wondering if trusting the policeman and going with the Japanese man had been the right decision.

Fretting fed my anxiety, and anxiety kindled doubt. The doubt was like a worm that gnawed at my hope and expectations. In order to stay strong, I needed some way to get rid of my worries.

They say that a smile brings good luck, so I should try to stay cheerful. Mom, I'm going to be heading to Japan soon. When I get my first month's pay at the textile mill, I'm going to send you all of it. I'm sorry I left without even saying goodbye, Mom!

During those fretful days, I tried to pass the time in pleasant daydreams.

I wonder how much money I'll make!

If I could save up all my pay month after month without spending any of it, I thought I'd be able to pay off my family's entire debt within the year. Once we were clear of that debt, I would stay frugal and keep saving money so I could treat my mom to a little luxury.

On our twelfth day at the inn, the Japanese man showed up and finally told the women to get in the truck. There were thirty-two of us by that point. After about an hour on the road, the truck stopped at an inn near Dongnae Station.

"Not another inn!"

"Just when are we actually going to Japan?"

Lifting one finger, the Japanese man told us to wait one more day. We were so excited that none of us got much sleep that night. The women who didn't speak Japanese fretted about how they were going to communicate once they got to Japan. Since I'd gone to elementary school, I could speak a little Japanese.

Early the next morning, the Japanese man told all the

women in the inn to come outside. Then he had ten of us, including me, stand off to one side and told us that only the others would be going to the docks to board a ship.

I was stunned, and the woman next to me spoke up. "Why aren't you taking us with you? You promised to get us jobs, too!"

The Japanese waved his hand dismissively and told us to wait for him at the inn. Tears formed in my eyes.

Why is he separating us out from the others?

The mystery was maddening. I tried to tell myself this would work out for the best.

There have got to be lots of factories in Japan. That must be why they didn't put us all on the same ship. Maybe my factory will turn out to be even better than the others. I've already waited over ten days, so one more day is no big deal.

As the women who were still at the inn tried to console each other, they became friends. The oldest woman there was named Jeong-ja. She felt bad for me because I was so young, so she made a point of looking after me.

Early that evening, the Japanese man came to get us.

See, there was no reason to be so worried. We must be headed somewhere different from the ones who left this morning.

The thought that we were finally going to Japan brought immediate relief from all my frustration. The Japanese man had us get in the truck.

I wonder how big our ship is going to be!

As soon as the truck pulled to a stop, we jumped out, excited to finally board the ship. But we weren't at the docks—we were in front of Dongnae Station.

We're supposed to be boarding a ship, so why are we here at the train station?

While we were looking around in confusion, the Japanese man came over. "You all are going to be taking the train. It's this way, so hurry up!"

He took us to the train, and before we had a chance to ask any questions, we were aboard.

We found ourselves in a long train car with a wooden floor and no seats. The windows were all draped in heavy olive green curtains, so we couldn't see outside. There were already a lot of other women in the train car.

"Can you take a train to Japan?" I asked Jeong-ja.

"No, the only way to get to Japan is by ship. It looks like they aren't taking us to Japan after all," Jeong-ja said, with worry in her voice.

Just then, a Japanese soldier standing by the door shouted at us to keep quiet. With a rifle in his arms, the soldier stared at us menacingly.

What's going on here?

I heard the clank of metal and guessed that the train

was on the move. Since we couldn't see out of the train, we had no idea where we were headed, which was really frustrating. From time to time, the train would emit a strange shriek, as if a wild beast were being strangled. It was only when the soldiers handed out rice balls and pickled radish that we knew it was dinner time.

Where could they be taking us?

I felt so nervous that it took me a while to get to sleep. Waking from a light doze, I saw a Japanese soldier dragging Jeong-ja toward the door of the train car.

I need Jeong-ja to be here with me! Where are they taking her?

I scrambled to my feet. "Jeong-ja! Where are you going?"

At that moment, another soldier shoved me with the butt of his rifle, which knocked me off my feet and sent me skidding along the wooden floor, in sheer terror. After sending Jeong-ja along to the next car, the soldier returned to his post by the door, as if nothing had happened. Jeong-ja had taken such good care of me, and I tossed and turned, hoping she would come back.

When I woke up the next morning, Jeong-ja was sprawled on the floor of the car.

"Jeong-ja! When did you get here? Where were you?"

But Jeong-ja only wept, with her face buried in the floor. All day long, her mind seemed elsewhere. She didn't even eat the rice ball she was given. Since the soldiers were watching us with nasty expressions on their faces, I didn't dare to ask her anything else.

On the evening of the third day, the train finally came to a halt. The doors opened, letting in a sharp gust of wind. A Japanese man came by and said that only the women who had boarded the train at Dongnae Station were supposed to alight there. The train station was too dark to see much of anything. Before long, a Japanese military truck pulled up, and once again we were loaded into the truck.

Where are we going this time?

The bed of the truck was covered by a canvas top. It was so dark outside I couldn't see a thing. I could barely remember how many days had passed since I left home. I felt like I was being dragged down a dark tunnel. It was so cold I couldn't think of anything else.

We must have been on the road for about two hours when I saw a faint gleam of light. The truck had pulled over at a Chinese inn. A woman in padded clothing came out and started jabbering as soon as she saw us. She must have been speaking Chinese, because I didn't understand a word of what she said. A man came over and told us in Korean to come inside. Jeong-ja asked him where we were. He told her we were in Manchuria.

I was startled to hear the name Manchuria. That was

where my dad had fought for Korea's independence from Japan.

Is Manchuria part of Japan, too, now?

When my little brother Chun-sik was three years old, my dad was away from home more often than not. When Chun-sik was six years old, I didn't see my dad at all and figured he was gone for good. But on cold winter days, my mom was sure to serve a bowl of rice for my dad at breakfast and dinner. She would put the bowl on the warmest spot of the floor and drape it with a blanket and then replace it with a new bowl at the next meal.

When Chun-sik was nine years old, I woke up early one morning to the sound of someone moving around. Opening my eyes, I saw that my dad was back. But I didn't recognize him at first, and not because it was dark. My dad had always been an ox of a man, strong enough to sling a big sack of rice over his shoulder. But now he trembled like a reed and could barely stay on his feet.

After returning home, my dad battled a persistent illness. My mom wouldn't say a word about where he'd been or what he'd done. My dad's body was racked by fever, and he was so fearful that a stiff breeze would startle him. The pitter-patter of mice in the ceiling at night was enough to make him stare around wildly.

My mom devoted herself to nursing my dad. That was when I dropped out of the elementary school I'd been going to. No matter how much medication my dad took, he didn't seem to get any better. We had to buy the drugs on credit at the pharmacy in town, and our debt kept growing.

There was a terrible drought that summer. This was even harder for Koreans to bear, since they were no longer the masters of their own country. The blazing sun shone down with relentless heat, as if determined to scorch the trees, the grass, and even the crops in the fields.

When the ears of the rice began to sprout, my dad was hauled to the police station. Someone who'd known him in Manchuria had gotten arrested and, under torture, blurted out that my father had been part of the independence movement there. That was when I found out my dad had been in Manchuria. Less than a week later, my father was sent home, a stone-cold corpse.

During the wake for my dad, Koreans and Japanese from the police station took turns monitoring everyone who came to pay their respects. Even our neighbors were so afraid of the police that they waited until dark to stop by.

The day we got my dad's body, the village was abuzz with the news that Sohn Kee-chung had won the gold medal in the marathon at the Berlin Olympics.

"Sohn Kee-chung is something else, isn't he? What an

amazing man!"

"He sure is! It's great to hear he's the world champion."

"It's a great feeling, but it's a crying shame, too. People around the world assume that Sohn is Japanese. He wore the Japanese flag when he ran."

"Seeing as the Japanese are running this place nowadays, there wasn't anything else he could've done."

"At any rate, Sohn has given us a reason to stand tall. I bet he sent a shiver down the spines of those Japanese!"

"Hush, everyone! That snitch who's working for the police is snooping around here again."

While some people were excited that Sohn Kee-chung had won the gold in the marathon, even more were embittered about it. Apparently, the Japanese flag had been pinned to Sohn's chest, instead of the Korean Taegeukgi, and the song that echoed through the skies above Berlin that day was the Japanese anthem "Kimigayo," not Korea's "Aegukga." For Koreans under the yoke of Japanese colonial rule, even good news was another reason to lament.

When the bier carrying my dad's body crested the hill on the way to our family's burial plot, my mom fainted, overwhelmed with grief. But she didn't have the luxury to grieve for long. The very next day, she went back to work so we could pay off our debt to the pharmacy. From that point forward, I was basically in charge of all the housework. All day long, I was kept busy going up the hill to gather firewood and then heading down to the fields to fill up jugs of water at the well. I even had to pick up stray ears of rice from the fields after the harvest.

When I went into town to deliver clothing my mom had sewn, I would head out to Ganwoldo Island to dig up some oysters to sell at the market along with dried greens that we'd gathered in the woods. But the money we earned from my mom's sewing and my trips to the market wasn't nearly enough to repay our debt. That's why the offer of a job at a Japanese textile mill was as welcome to me as a rain shower in a drought.

I went along with the Japanese man because I thought we were going to Japan, but now we're in Manchuria. Why would they have brought us all the way up here?

Even at the Chinese inn, the Japanese kept an eye on us. We were confined to our room, with little to do but wait for our chance to go to the textile mill. For our meals, the innkeeper brought us puréed soybean stew and rice balls mixed with millet.

I was restless, but time seemed to move at a crawl.

Eventually, I heard a car approaching. That was enough to pique my curiosity about what was going on and where we would be taken. Japanese soldiers came into the inn and handed out army fatigues. I'd set out on this journey in a flimsy black skirt and a white cotton jacket and hadn't been able to bring any extra clothes. So as soon as I was handed the fatigues, I pulled them over my other clothes.

Once we were dressed, the soldiers told us to get in the truck. It was so dark outside that I couldn't see my hands in front of me. The stars twinkled in the sky above me, making me miss home even more.

The truck set off again. The wind was starting to pick up, nipping at my skin. My body seemed to have frozen solid. If someone tapped me, I thought, I would snap in half like an icicle. My teeth were chattering, even though I was wearing the army fatigues on top of my other clothes.

How much farther is it to the textile mill?

The truck kept rattling along. To stay warm, I huddled together with the other women. Gray light peeked in through gaps in the truck's canvas shell. The day was breaking. The early morning wind pierced to the bone, and I could barely keep my eyes open.

How long have we been on the road?

The truck finally came to a stop. When the canvas shell was pulled back, I found myself facing a world covered in white snow. The soldiers yelled at us to get out of the truck, but we were too stiff to stand up right away. We had to rub our arms and legs for quite a while before we managed to climb down to the ground.

The sun was just coming up, and my eyes were dazzled by the sunlight reflected from the fields of snow. I could see a long row of buildings in front of us. The buildings were surrounded by a barbed wire fence, and armed Japanese soldiers were standing guard. The soldiers were dressed in fur caps and thick coats that revealed nothing but their glittering eyes.

A woman in a fur cap came over to us and led us into the largest building. In the middle of a huge hall was a stove, with a barrel of coal briquettes beside it. We gathered around the stove and held out our hands to warm them.

The woman removed her fur cap and began to speak. "Starting today, you'll be staying here with us. You can call me 'Auntie,' and you can call him 'Uncle,'" she said, pointing to a man beside her.

"Is this the textile mill?" I asked, but Auntie ignored my question and went on.

"The first thing you need to do is memorize your number. Your numbers will be assigned from youngest to oldest."

Auntie gave us our numbers. Since I was the youngest, I ended up being Number 1.

"You will now go to the room with your number on it," Uncle said gruffly. It was the voice of a soldier giving a command.

Auntie led us to our rooms and handed us some undergarments and dark olive baggy trousers before letting us inside. After taking a bath—my first in quite a while—I put on the new clothes I'd been given.

A Bird with Broken Wings

1937–1941, Inner Mongolia, China

Inside the room, I could see a wooden bed, a stove, a wooden bucket of water, a tiny kettle, and a small basin. Next to the basin was a bottle of pills.

Is this where I'm supposed to sleep?

Not long after, a bell rang outside. I cracked open the door and surveyed my surroundings. The women in the other rooms were all peering outside, just like me. A truck of soldiers had pulled up outside the barbed wire fence.

Auntie shouted at us to gather in the hall. I'd thought we were the only people in the camp, but there were a lot of women I didn't recognize. They were all from Korea.

"Where are we?" I asked a woman standing in front of me.

"This is Inner Mongolia," she said.

That didn't mean anything to me. "And what's 'Inner

Mongolia'?"

"It's just what they call this place. There's Russian territory over there, and there's a place called North Jiandao over that way. That's all we know."

"Where are the textile machines?"

Auntie cut me off. "Hush, everyone! Stop wasting your breath and eat your food!"

There was such a fierce expression on her face that I shut up at once. Standing in the front was a woman they called the group leader. She looked a little older than Jeong-ja. The group leader handed each of us a mess kit, like the ones the soldiers used. A Japanese soldier came in from the truck with a barrel full of cooked rice. The group leader dipped a big rice paddle into the barrel and scooped rice into our kits. Next to the group leader was a side dish container, the only options being miso soup and pickled plums. Standing there with my mess kit with the Japanese watching us so closely, I suddenly felt like an inmate.

What do they expect us to do in such a desolate place?

I was kicking myself for going off with that Japanese man so rashly.

I bet Mom and Chun-sik have been so anxious about finding me.

The thought that I should never have come here in the first place made the rice taste like gravel, even though I'd let it soak in the miso soup.

Part of me wanted to go outside and find out where the textile mill was, but I didn't dare move because of the military base nearby and the Japanese guards with their rifles. Even if there hadn't been any guards around, it was so cold outside I figured I'd probably freeze to death as soon as I stepped outside.

After I finished my meal and went back to my room, Auntie came in after me.

"Heo Chun-ja, as of today, your name is Haruko, Number 1."

I had no idea what she meant by that. "Huh? Why do I have to change my name? Is that a requirement for working at the textile mill?"

"The Japanese soldiers like Japanese names. Number 1 is Haruko, Number 2 is Fumiko, Number 3 is Akiko, Number 4 is Junko, and so on and so forth. So from now on, your name is Haruko, Number 1. Got it?"

As I stood there in bewilderment, Auntie pointed to the stove. "Only put in enough briquettes to keep the stove from going out."

As Auntie handed me a blanket, she frowned at me, a doubtful look in her eyes. "Since you're so young, Haruko, a special soldier is going to visit you tonight. As long as you do what he says, nothing will happen. But if you try to resist, he might beat you. You need to be accommodating and attentive."

"Why is a special soldier coming here? When am I going to start working at the factory?"

I had so many questions to ask. Why had they given us separate rooms instead of having us share them? Where on earth was the factory and when were we going to start working there? I was curious about everything.

"You're the only one getting this special treatment. Starting tomorrow, you'll be like everyone else. Just try to make it through the night. Every time a Japanese soldier leaves, you have to dissolve one of those pills in the water and wash yourself down below."

What was she rambling on about now? Why would she tell me to wash my legs and feet?

"Auntie, just a moment," I broke in as she opened the door to go. "Where's the textile mill?"

At that, Auntie spun back around. "There's no textile mill here. In a little while, the soldiers will be coming in, so don't leave your room. Have you got that?"

Then she left, slamming the door behind her.

So I'm supposed to be accommodating to this special soldier? And there's no textile mill? In that case, why did they bring me here? And what did she mean about nothing happening if I do as the soldier says?

I paced up and down for a while and then sat down on the wooden bed. It felt very cold, so I laid down the blanket Auntie had given me. Raising the lid of the stove, I tossed in one of the coal briquettes. When the fire reached the little black lump, it released a bluish flame.

After a little while, there was a commotion outside. I heard the tramp of boots and doors being yanked open and slammed shut.

I wonder what Jeong-ja is doing right now.

My curiosity got the better of me, and I pushed on the door. But the door was locked.

Auntie must have locked it from the outside.

Since there weren't any windows in the room, I strained my ears and tried to figure out what was happening outside. From time to time, I heard crying and screaming. With every passing minute, I got more and more nervous.

What do the textile mill, the Japanese soldiers, and this tiny room have to do with each other?

I had no idea why I had to wait for a Japanese soldier I'd never met before. I felt as fearful as if I were wandering through a dark forest by myself in the middle of the night.

After quite some time, I heard heavy footsteps right in front of my door. It looked as if the soldier I was waiting for had finally arrived. I had no clue what I was supposed to do. Should I stand up or sit down? Should I stay quiet or say hello?

I heard a key turning in the lock. A moment later, the door flung open, and a Japanese soldier stepped into the room. He was holding a kerosene lamp, and two gold stars on his shoulders glittered in its flickering light. Inside the room, the soldier pulled off his fur hat and grinned at me, which for some reason gave me the chills.

Perhaps this soldier is special because he's wearing stars.

The soldier looked a little younger than my dad had been. He was fairly short, with an average build. He had a rifle in his hand and a long sword at his waist.

The soldier put his rifle on the floor and laid his sword down next to the bed. I was too frightened to look at him directly and took a sidelong glance at his face. He had a mustache and fierce-looking narrow eyes. He took a seat on the bed and asked me to take off his boots. Unable to disobey, I took them off and then went to stand in the corner of the room.

The soldier held out his hand, gesturing for me to come to the bed. I shook my head. He reached out and grabbed my arm and yanked me toward him. In terror, I tried to open the door and run out, but before I could, his heavy hand struck me in the back and knocked me to the floor.

The soldier lifted me up and flung me onto the bed like a rag doll. I didn't understand what was going on.

Did I do something wrong?

I wrung my hands together pitifully, begging the soldier to stop. But he held out his hand and curtly ordered me to stand up.

I hurriedly got to my feet, and the soldier held out his hands toward me. This time, his voice was softer. "Come over here."

Out of fright, I took a step backward. My whole body was trembling.

If he'd told me to put some coal in the stove or wash his feet, I think I could've managed that much. There was a fire burning in the soldier's eyes, and I could feel it getting hotter. All of a sudden, he lifted me into the air and threw me back onto the bed. In his harsh grip, the most I could do was squirm and wiggle like a worm. The soldier tried to tear off my jacket. With a cry, I pushed against his chest as hard as I could. His powerful hands yanked at the two sides of my jacket until the string holding them together snapped. His hot breath blasted my face, like steam from the nostrils of an angry bull.

I covered my chest with my hands and screamed. "Somebody, help me!"

A flash of light filled my vision—the soldier had slapped me across the face. When I tried to wriggle out of his grasp, there was another flash of light, and then a second and a third.

"Stupid girl!"

The soldier's hot and hideous breath enveloped my face, and his body weighed down on me like a millstone. I could barely breathe. I fought back with all my strength, but I was like a caterpillar pinned under a boulder. The soldier held down my shoulder with one hand and fondled my breasts with the other.

Why is he doing this to me? What does he want?

I suddenly saw my mother's face.

She always told me to watch myself around men. Is this what Auntie meant by 'special treatment'?

I pushed back as hard as I could, but that just made the soldier grope me all the more. I screamed my lungs out for Auntie to come help me, but she didn't come. Before long, those vile hands reached my underpants. A serpent seemed to have wrapped itself around my body. Despite my best effort to free myself, the soldier held me down while he lowered his pants with his free hand.

There's got to be some way to get this monster away from me!

While I was hysterically jerking my head from side to side and screaming for help, the edge of my mouth came into contact with the soldier's wrist, just above the hand that was holding down my shoulder. In desperation, I chomped down on his wrist. With a roar, he staggered to his feet. As he cradled his wrist in his free hand, he stared wildly around, like a raging wild boar. Then he picked up the rifle and brought the stock crashing down on my head. After an instant of terrible pain, I blacked out.

Someone was slapping me. Opening my eyes, I saw Auntie and began to wail. I wanted to ask her why she'd waited so long, to tell her I felt like I was going to die. But I was shaking so hard and in so much pain that the words just wouldn't come out. Auntie dipped a towel into the bucket of water and wiped my head. The towel came away smeared with blood. When I'd had a moment to collect my thoughts, I realized I was stark naked. I hurriedly pulled the blanket over my body. There was a searing pain in my private parts.

"Foolish girl! I told you to be accommodating, didn't I? Do you have a death wish? Why did you fight back?"

Auntie's voice was cutting and menacing, but there wasn't anyone else I could turn to.

"Auntie, why did the soldier do that to me? I'm scared. I don't like this. The textile mill—"

Auntie broke in before I could finish. "Thank your lucky stars you're still alive! If that had been any ordinary soldier, you would've been dead meat. Why did you bite him on the wrist, like a rabid dog?"

Auntie rubbed some red ointment on my head. "Heat up some water in the kettle and rinse off your privates with that. Be sure to mix in one of those pills; that's the disinfectant."

"What a stupid girl," Auntie muttered on her way out of the room. She shut the door with a bang.

I could barely manage to get out of bed. My crotch was drenched in blood, and my privates hurt so badly I couldn't stand up straight.

What on earth did that man do to me?

The room spun around me and my legs folded, sending me tumbling back onto the bed. I needed to pee. When I tried squatting down, I felt a terrible pain in my groin. I thought of that beast of a soldier. I could remember everything that had happened until he struck me on the head with his rifle, but nothing after that. With an effort, I managed to relieve myself and get dressed. It felt like filthy bugs were crawling over my breasts, over my whole body. I poured some of the hot water from the kettle into the basin and then took one of the pills out of the bottle and dissolved it in the water. The water turned as pink as an azalea, but there was nothing beautiful about it.

I painfully scrubbed down every inch of my body. I cleaned my breasts, my belly button, my thighs, and my hands. Tears streamed down my face.

Why did I follow that Japanese man?

With every movement, blood dripped from between my legs.

Death might be better than this.

My head was throbbing, too. Gingerly touching my scalp, I found my hair was matted with congealed blood. The room was bitterly cold, but I didn't even have the strength to put a briquette in the stove. All I could do was pull the blanket over myself and curl up, trying to endure the pain, between bouts of sobbing.

I want to go home, Mom. What do I do now?

The whole story about the textile mill was hateful to me. If that policeman who'd promised to get me a job had been there in front of me, I would've sunk my teeth into him.

Am I the only one in this situation? Is Jeong-ja OK?

My teeth were chattering, and I was shivering all over. Once again, I blacked out.

Someone was shaking me violently. When I managed to open my eyes, I saw Auntie. The morning had come.

"Didn't you hear the bell? Do you mean to starve to death? Hurry along with your mess kit!"

Auntie put a briquette in the stove and pushed the mess kit toward me. But I couldn't get up. I hadn't even heard the bell.

Auntie rapped the mess kit with the briquette scooper,

pressing me to go eat. I shook my head. I wasn't in the mood to eat, and I didn't think I could keep anything down, anyway.

"Do you know how much money went into you? Hurry and get up!"

About all I could manage to do was roll over in bed.

What is this money she's talking about?

Auntie carried my mess kit out with her and returned with some rice, which she flung down on my bed before leaving once more. Even the aroma of the rice was nauseating. The pain in my groin was unbearable. I was thirsty, but I didn't dare drink any water because I might have to go to the bathroom. I couldn't stop shaking, but I pulled myself to my feet and added a briquette to the stove.

After a while, Auntie came back to the room. "Why aren't you eating your food? Do you want to make things hard for us, or are you just suicidal? Starting today, you're just like any other *josenpi*. The soldiers will be showing up any minute now, so hurry up and eat your food!"

Josenpi? I hadn't heard that word before. The news that more Japanese soldiers were on their way hit me like a knife in the gut.

"I can't do it, Auntie. This pain is killing me. Please don't let the soldiers into my room. I'm begging you! The only reason I came was to work at the textile mill."

"How can you be so stupid, Haruko? Do you still not know why you're here?"

"I was brought here by a Japanese man who told me I would be working at a textile mill. You can send me to the factory, right?"

"Just shut up! This is a comfort station for the Japanese army. Do you understand? You're just a *josenpi*. You're a comfort woman for the Japanese soldiers. Have you got that?"

I threw my arms around Auntie's baggy pants and pleaded with her. "No, that can't be true. There's been some kind of mistake. I wouldn't have come here if I'd known it would be like this."

There was a tearing pain in my groin, and more blood dribbled down my calves. The blood made me even more scared.

"Can you please send me home, Auntie? Please?"

The older woman lost her temper. "You stupid girl! Do you think anyone would come if they were told the truth? All the girls were tricked into coming here, just like you. Do you even know where we are right now? We're in Inner Mongolia, hundreds of miles from Korea. If you want to stay alive, you need to keep your mouth shut. If you get on the soldiers' nerves, they'll step on you like a bug. A little bleeding down there isn't going to kill you. You'll get used to everything after a while. Hurry up and eat. If you're accommodating and agreeable and stop being stupid, you won't get hit. That's the way to stay alive."

As Auntie strode out of the room, I just shook my head. I couldn't let those awful soldiers have their way with me. I tried to put Auntie's words out of my head.

I wanted to run away and go somewhere else, anywhere else. I struggled to my feet and opened the door. In every direction, the landscape was covered in snow. I couldn't see anywhere to hide. For me, the white blanket of snow was a shroud of darkness. In exhaustion, I closed the door again. For now, anyway, the pain in my groin was so bad I could barely walk, let alone run away.

As I watched the steaming rice grow cold, I began to cry again. The more I cried, the worse my headache got where I'd been hit by the rifle butt. I lay back down on the bed and pulled the covers above my head. I never wanted to wake up again.

What exactly went wrong? Why was I brought here to suffer like this?

It made me shudder to think that the vile soldiers were about to come back and do what the soldier had done to me the day before. I felt a wild longing to see my mom and Chun-sik. My headache gradually got worse, and I lay there groaning until I finally passed out.

All at once, the door was thrown open by a Japanese soldier I'd never seen before. Coming into the room, he laid his gun down next to the bed and propped his sword against the wall. I jumped to my feet, my pain forgotten. I crouched down in the corner and raised my hands in a cry for help. The soldier picked me up and flung me onto the bed, just like the day before. I tossed my head and tried to resist. I frantically shouted that I was in too much pain, that I was bleeding that very moment. But the pitiless soldier forced my legs open. The room echoed with my screams of agony. Stop this, I shouted, it hurts so much. But my screams faded and at last my voice gave out.

The Japanese soldier slapped me savagely. He was an awful fiend, a slavering beast with glinting eyes. The more I fought him, the coarser his panting became. I wanted to bite the fiend's hand as I had last time, but with his constant slapping, he didn't give me a chance. I fought for dear life; that was all I could do. The soldier leapt to his feet and seized his sword, swinging it around until the cruel gleaming steel rested against my neck. If I moved an inch, I thought, the blade would slice into my neck. I froze in place, unable to move. The soldier at last put his sword down, but seemed ready to pick it back up at any time.

I squeezed my eyes shut. I thought it would be better to die than endure this. The fiend, the beast, climbed back on top of me.

I'd rather die!

I gritted my teeth and held my breath. I felt a pain between my legs, as if my insides were being carved out with a knife, and then I passed out. Faintly, I thought I could hear the door opening. Another beast came in and raped me. It was an awful nightmare. A herd of grotesque beasts assaulted me, one after another. The soldiers toyed with me, as if I were their plaything.

Several days went by like that. Physically, I was a wreck, and mentally, I was barely there. I couldn't tell what time it was or even whether it was day or night. I spooned rice into my mouth automatically and swallowed it out of habit. I wanted to forget how to think, to forget what was happening. I was ashamed to even be alive.

Every numbered room was a place where those monsters raped us every day. It was no use to cry out, struggle, or resist. Each and every day was hell, and in that hell we were made to feel shame and live like the dead.

Every day we spent in that living hell, Jeong-ja and the other women cried until they were hoarse, just like me, and their bodies were lined with bruises, just like me. The assault on our genitals was relentless, leaving them no time to heal. I had the hardest time of it because I was so young. My vagina became so swollen that I couldn't even pee, which made me bloated. Whenever I ran into Jeong-ja, she cried at the sight of me. She was so horrified that even her crying sounded twisted, broken, and mangled.

A few days later, a doctor came by the comfort station. He was part of the Japanese army, too. The army doctor gave us medical exams in a storage room next to Auntie's room. He had brought a peculiar wooden chair with stirrups on it. When I sat in the chair and put my feet in the stirrups, my legs spread wide and revealed my private parts. The army doctor told Auntie that my genitals had been torn because I was so young and that I shouldn't service any more soldiers until my wounds had healed.

For about five days, the number tag hanging from my door was turned over, which let the Japanese soldiers know they couldn't come in.

I was standing at a crossroads, unsure whether I should keep going or just give up. There was no point in running away in this desolate country, since I was sure to be caught. I was like a trapped bird that couldn't fly. I was a bird with broken wings. For my entire first year at the comfort station, my frozen heart felt as cold as the winter in Inner Mongolia.

The next spring, when the snow and ice had started to melt, one of the women at the comfort station disappeared without a trace. Auntie and the Japanese soldiers searched the area around the comfort station with a fine-toothed comb, but they couldn't find her.

"It's like she just vanished into thin air. If she did escape from the comfort station, she was probably gobbled down by the wolves," Auntie said. She grumbled about all the money she was losing with one fewer woman to entertain the Japanese soldiers.

Several days later, a corpse turned up in the outhouse, floating up from the pit below the toilet. I couldn't stand to look at the body, which was caked yellow with excrement. It was the woman who had supposedly run away. Starting that very day, Auntie kept an eye on us even when we went to the bathroom.

That was the first of three women at the comfort station who died in less than a year. The second woman slit her wrists. When they found her the next morning, her body was already cold. The third woman to die was Jeong-ja, the one who'd always looked after me. She'd come down with some horrible disease that caused her crotch to rot.

Time proved a remarkable medicine. As the months went by, I gained the strength to suppress my feelings of both hatred and sadness, intense as they were. Those who couldn't put up with their sadness and desperation became more and more depressed and eventually resorted to suicide. But I was so upset with the Japanese for how they'd tricked and abused me that I was determined not to die.

At mealtime one day, one of the women who had come with me to Inner Mongolia showed me a hairpin that a Japanese soldier had given her.

"This would look really good on you, Haruko! I'm too old to wear a hairpin like this. Lean over and I'll pin it on you."

As the woman was about to put the hairpin in my hair, I remembered the ribbon I'd used to wear on my braid, the hair the Japanese had cut off.

During the first physical we received after arriving in Inner Mongolia, Auntie had lopped off our long braids and given us bob cuts. The memory of that moment ignited a fireball of emotion in my gut. Snatching the hairpin away from the other woman, I flung it onto the ground and stamped on it.

"Whoa, wait a minute! That's a valuable hairpin!"

"Don't you women have any self-respect? What's so great about a hairpin you got from a Japanese soldier? You want me to put *that* in my hair?"

My chest heaving, I crushed the hairpin under my shoe. For a moment, silence hung over the room.

One of the other women spoke up. "Haruko's right. The Japanese deserve every bit of our hatred."

The woman who'd given me the hairpin was angry now,

too, and her face blushed with anger. "Yeah, I don't know what I was thinking. I guess you have to be a little crazy to put up with all this. If I focused on what life is like here, I couldn't last a single day. The unfairness of it all makes me sick. But dying wouldn't change anything. I just have to hang on until this is over. I've got to stay alive until I get back home. They tricked me into coming here, and I'm not going to die in this place."

Finally, the woman broke down and wept. All the women around us were crying, and I was sobbing alongside them. Having a good cry seemed to relieve some of the tension inside.

Another year passed in this way. One day, a young soldier who couldn't have been older than twenty came into my room. I'd always managed to endure the soldiers' visits by telling myself that they were animals, not people. As usual, I lay back with my eyes shut, hoping the soldier would hurry up and get it over with. When I didn't hear anything, I opened my eyes and saw the soldier gazing at me.

"How old are you?" he asked me.

For a moment, I couldn't believe my ears. None of the soldiers had ever spoken to me in Korean before. I jumped to my feet without realizing it and then blushed with embarrassment.

"I'm Korean, and I grew up in Tongyeong. Where are

you from?"

"Sir," I said, but couldn't get any further. Just hearing this soldier speaking to me in my own language made me weep. The man from Tongyeong patted me on the back and clucked his tongue in sympathy.

I held on to him. "Sir, can you please take me with you? Anywhere is fine, as long as there aren't any Japanese soldiers there. Just get me out of here!"

"They're awful, aren't they?" he said. "But tell me, where are you from?"

"I'm from Seosan. My name is Heo Chun-ja. Not Haruko, but Heo Chun-ja!" When I said my name, hot tears rolled down my cheeks.

"All right, I know how hard this must be. You've got to stay strong and persevere. That's the only way to get home alive. Don't cry. I'll visit you again."

The man from Tongyeong stood to his feet, but I clung desperately to him.

"Please don't leave me here."

"I can't help it. There are Japanese soldiers waiting outside. If I stay too long, they'll throw a fit. I'll be back."

Just then, a Japanese soldier waiting outside kicked the door and swore. When the man from Tongyeong stepped outside, I heard the Japanese soldier curse at him. And then a swarm of Japanese soldiers descended on my room.

Every day after that, I looked forward to seeing the man from Tongyeong. It was the first time since arriving at that horrible place that I'd looked forward to seeing anyone. The man from Tongyeong visited once a week. Whenever he came, we would talk about our hometowns. He sometimes felt so sorry for me that he would cry with me. Sometimes he told me stories about the battlefield, and at other times he brought me sweets.

One day, the man from Tongyeong had some honey with him. "Here, I brought this for you. It was hard to get my hands on this."

"Let's eat it together."

"Since being drafted for the war, I've lost so much weight. I bet my own mother couldn't recognize me now. I brought this honey for you because you're as skinny as a toothpick. You need to eat a lot if you want to stay strong," he said, clucking his tongue.

"You know, I used to be chubby, too."

"Yeah, I bet! Anyhow, you need to always take care of yourself. Don't let yourself get sick. The Japanese won't give you any medical treatment, and if you die, they'll just chuck you out with the trash. So try to get enough to eat."

"I will. I appreciate you telling me that."

The genuine concern in the man's voice brought tears to my eyes. While I was with him, I felt more like the girl I'd

Trampled Blossoms

been before leaving home. He also made me miss Jin-gyu, the boy from my village.

I'd never felt as happy as when I was waiting for the next visit by this man who appreciated me, sympathized with me, and understood me. But my happiness didn't last. Before long, the man from Tongyeong was sent back to his original unit. After he left, I went back to being Haruko, living in a hell with no one to call me by my real name.

As the months passed, I became acclimated to Inner Mongolia and its bleak and biting wind and the sandstorms blowing through its desolate and treeless wasteland. This was a land where flowers bloomed sideways because the roaring north wind kept the grass from growing straight. But every day, I was trampled upon and kept from blossoming like the wildflowers all around me.

I spent four years in the demons' den of that Japanese comfort station as ghostly Haruko, thin as a reed and in a mental daze.

Driven by the Bitter Wind

From Nanjing to Shanghai, 1941

One evening, a convoy of trucks abruptly pulled up at the base and hurriedly loaded up equipment and soldiers. The man and woman who ran the comfort station—who were basically stooges for the Japanese army—urged us to pack our things.

"Get your stuff together. We're leaving here tonight," Auntie said.

"Where are we going?"

"Who knows? We have to follow the Japanese soldiers wherever they go."

On orders from the Japanese, we boarded a truck with Auntie and Uncle.

Everything I owned fit into a single bundle. All I had was a dented powder case (we were given one each year) and a wad of tattered clothing (rags, really) that I used when I was on my period. We crouched down in the truck, cradling our bundles of clothing like a priceless treasure. Before I knew it, my mind had wandered back to my home, hundreds of miles away.

Because the truck bed was covered by a canvas roof, I couldn't see anything outside. The Japanese troops always moved us around in military trucks with canvas roofs and kept us under close surveillance, just as when they'd first brought us there.

The trucks set off in a long line, kicking up clouds of sand and dust. We seemed to be driven by the bitter wind that races over the desolate wasteland of Inner Mongolia, swift as a tiger. I'd come to hate that monotonous landscape, and it brought me a keen joy to bid it farewell.

As the road brought new sights that were soon replaced by others, I found myself thinking back to my younger years. When I'd left home at the age of thirteen, I'd been as delicate as a budding flower. The thought of my beloved home, which I feared I'd never see again, always brought tears to my eyes. I also cried when I thought of my mom and Chun-sik. If I could just go back to our cozy life together, I felt, I wouldn't need anything else. I missed the skies, the winds, and the clouds of my childhood, and I would gladly have accepted total poverty if only I could be home again. The other women and I fervently hoped that this journey would end at our homes.

The more I missed home, the more I resented my sad lot: my budding flower had been trampled into the dirt, and I'd never be able to blossom again. But we comforted ourselves with the thought that not being able to blossom or bear fruit didn't mean we weren't trees. We told ourselves that even the trees without fruit or flowers boldly lift their branches into the sky, giving the birds a place to build their nests.

At mealtime, the Japanese soldiers would share a little of their military rations with us, though it didn't satisfy our hunger. They gave us just enough to keep us from starving. On some days, we would eat radishes that we'd picked on the side of the road. On other days, the soldiers would stop the truck next to a field of unripe sorghum and have us pick the ears of grain for our meal. When it grew dark, we would be let out of the truck to relieve ourselves in an empty field or way out in the woods.

After several days of passing through endless plains, our truck stopped at a tiny village. Once we were out of the truck, I realized that the village was Chinese. We had parked by a sandy beach near the mouth of a river. I could see several army trucks that were of the same sort as ours. There were also some tank trucks carrying gas. Soldiers had removed the tires from one of the trucks and were crawling around underneath it to make repairs. All the women had to stay inside the truck. We ate our meals there and slept there as well.

Even when night fell, no lights came on in the village, and there wasn't a soul to be seen. I wasn't sure whether the villagers were hunkering down because of the Japanese soldiers or whether the village had been deserted before they came.

The next day, we were joined by more trucks. Every time another convoy arrived, there was a truck full of women.

Late at night on our third day in the village, the silence was broken by gunfire. There was an explosion right in front of our truck.

"Hit the ground!" said a Japanese soldier, brandishing his gun at us.

We lay there in the truck bed, staying perfectly still. I was afraid that I'd be shot if I so much as lifted my head. Around sunrise, when the sky grew light, the gunfire stopped and gave way to silence.

"They say we were ambushed by bandits," one of the women whispered as we lay there. I found myself hoping that even more bandits would attack the Japanese. Apparently, several of the trucks had caught on fire, and a number of Japanese soldiers had been injured, too.

A Japanese officer came over to our truck and asked

Auntie to come out. I may not have cared for her very much, but she was our only guardian. Anxiously, I wondered what was going on.

After a while, Auntie came back and called to me. "Haruko, go with that officer."

My heart was pounding, but I tried to stay calm as I walked behind him. We soon reached a makeshift tent with cots set up inside. There were injured soldiers lying on the cots, and a few women were bandaging their legs.

Someone said the soldiers had been shot by the bandits. There were plenty of times I would've gladly shot a Japanese soldier, if only I'd had a gun. There were plenty of things I would've liked to do, if not for the armed soldiers standing watch.

The army doctor kept me busy running errands: fetch some water, mix the disinfectant, clean the wounds. I wiped blood from the wounds and dressed them.

I wonder why Auntie trusted me enough to have me take care of the soldiers.

Seeing the soldiers moaning in agony, I had trouble holding back the urge to torture them the way they'd tortured me. One of these days, I worried, the volcano of rage that was building up inside me might just erupt.

These people are in pain, so of course I ought to help them. I'm not like the Japanese. I'm a good person!

As I cleaned the soldiers' wounds and tried to keep my rage in check, a woman who looked a bit older than me walked over, holding some bandages. There was kindness and warmth in her round face, and an unusual depth in her eyes. I was suddenly reminded of Jeong-ja, who was gone forever. I greeted the older woman with a nod. Her deep eyes were filled with fear.

The woman was leaning over to dress the injured soldier's leg when he reached up and grabbed one of her breasts. She shrieked in shock. For a moment, the soldier looked like one of the men who'd raped me. Before I could stop myself, I smacked his hand as hard as I could. I guess my hatred gave that smack some extra zing, because the soldier yelped with pain and rubbed his hand.

The woman seized that opportunity to hurriedly straighten out her rumpled clothing. The army doctor came running over to see what had happened. With a look of fear on her face, the woman pointed at the injured soldier. The soldier told the doctor I'd hit him. Infuriated, I said that the soldier had actually tried to rape the other woman.

The doctor seemed to have figured out what had happened. After glaring first at me and then at the soldier, he yelled, "You idiot!"

I wasn't sure whether he was talking to me or to the soldier.

After a moment, the doctor told me to disinfect some of his tools with alcohol and then went to take care of another wounded soldier. When he stepped away from us, the other woman spoke to me.

"Thanks a lot. I was worried the doctor was going to shoot you!"

"I didn't even mean to hit that guy."

"You're really lucky it was the doctor. An ordinary soldier would have shot you dead on the spot."

It was only then that I realized how much of a risk I'd taken.

I was about to fetch some more water when the woman asked me a question. "So where did you come from anyway?"

"Inner Mongolia."

"Inner Mongolia? I mean, where did you grow up?"

"Seosan, in Chungcheong Province."

"I'm from Jinju, in Gyeongsang Province. My name is Bok-sun, and my Japanese name is Fumiko. What about you?"

"I'm Chun-ja, and my Japanese name is Haruko."

"I was at a comfort station in Nanjing. When did you leave Korea?"

"Four years ago."

"OK, we'll talk again when we have a chance. In the

meantime, we should act like we don't know each other."

"All right."

In front of the doctor, Bok-sun and I didn't say a word to each other. We waited until he was at a distance, and even then only spoke in whispers.

"If you came here four years ago, how old were you at the time?"

"I was thirteen. What about you?"

"I was eighteen when they brought me here. I stayed in Nanjing for two years and turned twenty this year. Have you started having a period?"

"Yeah, I had my first one this year."

"What a world we live in," Bok-sun muttered. The next moment, the army doctor called her name.

"Watch out. I'll talk to you soon."

From then on, Bok-sun took me under her wing.

After five days in the Chinese ghost town, the Japanese troops resumed their journey. Bok-sun and I rode in the truck with the wounded soldiers. It was a great comfort just having her there with me. Surrounded as we were by the injured and by our guards, most of our communication was nonverbal.

While the Japanese soldiers were out of the truck, Bok-sun managed to tell me about what she'd gone through in Nanjing. Around the time I was being transported to Inner

Mongolia, Japan had started a war with China. After capturing Shanghai, the Japanese army had attacked the Chinese capital of Nanjing and slaughtered hundreds of thousands of Chinese.

"Where are we going? I asked Bok-sun. "I wish they'd take us back home."

"That would be great, wouldn't it? What I hear is that we're close to Shanghai."

Right then, the soldiers came back into the truck. We spun around and pretended not to know each other.

About ten days after leaving Inner Mongolia, we finally arrived at Shanghai. It was a huge metropolis, a different world altogether from the barren plains of Inner Mongolia. I could see tall buildings and alleys bustling with bicycles and rickshaws. But many of the buildings we passed were in ruins. The corner had collapsed on one building, and the roof had caved in on another. Some of the walls were riddled with bullet holes.

Our truck passed out of the city center and stopped close to the shore, where we could see the ocean. Dozens of Japanese military trucks were already assembled there.

Monsters in My Room

Yangjiazhai comfort station, 1941

As soon as our truck reached the shore, Japanese soldiers came over to count the number of women inside. Auntie handed the soldiers a piece of paper for them to check, which I guessed was a list of our names.

"Bok-sun, it looks like they're about to send us home," I said, after making sure that none of the soldiers were watching.

"Do you think so? I really hope you're right."

After a while, the soldiers took us to another truck. There were already a lot of women inside, along with two soldiers in the front and two more in the back who were assigned to watch us.

The truck left the shore and drove for quite a long time into the city. The only way to get home was by ship, and the fact that we were heading back into town dashed my hopes.

Once we'd left the busy downtown area, the truck drove along quiet streets for a while until we reached a long row of army barracks. At both entrances, there were large signs in Japanese.

Bok-sun leaned over and whispered in my ear. "The signs say, 'A big welcome to the warriors fighting the holy war.'"

"Are they welcoming us?"

"No, it's for the Japanese soldiers."

Just then, one of the soldiers in our truck yelled at everyone to shut up.

Across the way, there was another big banner. That one also bore a message in Japanese, written from top to bottom.

Bok-sun cocked her head. "'Sacred latrine for the Imperial Army'?"

"What does that mean"?

Bok-sun hushed me.

When the truck came to a stop, the Japanese soldiers told us to hurry out. Two strangers, a man and woman in baggy pants, came over and counted us. There were thirty-five of us altogether.

The woman took us into one of the barracks buildings. The building was divided into more than twenty separate rooms. Hanging on each of the doors was something all too familiar to us—number tags.

This comfort station was much bigger than the one in Inner Mongolia. While I was wondering why such a big station would be located so close to the docks, I remembered the dozens of Japanese trucks I'd seen by the shore. I was worried that those soldiers would congregate on the comfort station all at once.

The rooms in our building were lined up like rabbit hutches. Each room contained a bed, a water bucket, a basin, and some disinfectants. Sure enough, the Japanese had brought us there to do that same disgusting job. We weren't people, but mere numbers. I was Number 25, and Bok-sun was Number 26.

Meals were served in a cafeteria in the middle of each building. The one where Bok-sun and I stayed was run by a Japanese couple. The man looked rather unsavory, but the woman could speak Korean. Just as before, we called them Auntie and Uncle.

We began receiving Japanese soldiers the next day. From morning until evening, crowds of soldiers thronged to the comfort station, which was called Yangjiazhai. In Inner Mongolia, I'd never had to service more than fifteen soldiers in one day, but here the average was thirty; on busy days, there were more than forty.

Looking back, the days when I hadn't dealt with soldiers

during the trip from Inner Mongolia to Shanghai felt like paradise. Bok-sun told me that, while she was being transported in a truck in Nanjing, the soldiers had hung up a screen and raped her then and there.

The stream of men I serviced each day included soldiers, sailors, military doctors, and even high-ranking civilians working for the army. During the day, it was typically enlisted men, while at night, it would be officers. Sometimes these officers would spend the night at the comfort station and not leave until the next morning.

Day after day, the lines of soldiers grew longer. The longer the lines, the more violent the soldiers became. Even a brief wait was enough to make them cause a scene. They were no better than beasts. They would kick the door and spew profanities, yelling at the soldier before them to hurry up.

Every day, it seemed like soldiers were coming from different units. All of them behaved like animals, as if they'd never been with a woman before. Within less than a month, my body was swollen, torn, and bruised. I often fainted from the unbearable pain. Some soldiers would beat me simply because they didn't get the response they wanted.

After a month, we were loaded into army trucks and taken to a naval hospital. The doctor said I had a severe inflammation and couldn't take any soldiers for three days. I had to do laundry at the hospital instead. Most of the women working there were comfort women like me. When they had a condition that kept them from servicing soldiers, they were assigned to do laundry or dress the wounded. I managed to get a lot of information out of these women.

The women at the hospital told me that Japan had occupied China and was about to launch an even bigger war. It was to prepare for that war that Japanese troops from various areas had assembled at Shanghai. A lot of Japanese troops were anxious about the war, and a large comfort station had been set up to bring them relief. Many Chinese women had also been kidnapped to work at the station. I was even more shocked to learn that the Japanese army referred to the comfort stations as their "sacred latrines." I remembered how Bok-sun had been taken aback by the big sign hanging in front of Yangjiazhai comfort station when we first got there.

Sacred latrines! Do those awful soldiers think the body my parents gave me is some kind of toilet where they can relieve themselves of their carnal desires?

Before I knew it, I was grinding my teeth.

Returning to the comfort station after spending three days at the hospital felt like walking back into the gates of hell. Whenever a soldier was on top of me, my survival technique was pretending to be dead. But when I thought of the phrase "sacred latrine," I couldn't hold back a shudder. It may not have been apparent from the outside, but my body would go rigid, as if my rage had shut down all the cells in my body.

As time went by, the Japanese soldiers became more unruly and seemed to be going insane. Without warning, they would brutally punch or kick me. Some didn't like my facial expression, and others were disappointed because I didn't seem excited. Some thought I was putting on airs; and still others just weren't having a good time. All this wound up the rage inside me ever more tightly, and I was worried that I would snap someday.

One day, a Japanese soldier came into my room wearing insignia I'd never seen before. Whereas the regular soldiers wore a rank badge with stars on a red background, this one had stars on a gold bar.

As soon as the soldier entered the room, he told me to take my clothes off. Like it or not, disobedience wasn't an option. With trembling hands, I removed my military fatigues. When I was about to get into bed, the soldier ran forward and started tearing up my clothing. Before I could help myself, I shrieked.

"That's good. Louder!" the soldier yelled as he threw a punch at me. This wasn't a man, but a monster.

The anger I'd kept trapped inside burst out. "What was that for? Why are you hitting me?"

With a snigger, the monster hit me even harder. "Good, that's very good! I want you to howl even louder, like a savage wolf pup!"

In that moment, I was horrified by my predicament. The monster was beating me to get a rise out of me and then taking pleasure from seeing me scream with pain and frustration. It made me furious. The moment I realized that freak was getting off on my reaction, I stopped screaming. My veins bulged as I strained to hold back my anger.

How I'd love to hurl myself on that monster's naked body and tear off his flesh with my teeth! Maybe there's some way I could take him down with me.

As the anger blazed hotter in my eyes, the monster pummeled me even harder. My whole body trembled as rage coursed through me, from my head to my toes. Then my vision went white and I collapsed, unconscious.

By the time I came to my senses, the monster was already gone. I was sprawled on the floor of my room, with my clothes torn to ribbons. I figured it was probably best that I'd blacked out.

That afternoon, a bell tolled in the field outside. Something horrible happened every time that bell tolled.

I wonder what's going to happen today!

I felt uneasy as Uncle led us out onto the field.

A woman was lying on the field. Her messy hair hung

limply, concealing her face. Her torn clothing was red with blood. A Japanese soldier was jabbing the woman with his sword. His hand was wrapped in a bandage. The moment I saw the soldier's rank badge, I sucked in my breath and shivered with fear. It was the very monster who'd been in my room! I hurriedly ducked my head.

The monster shouted, "We are the holy army of His Imperial Majesty! You are *josenpi*, and you exist to serve the Imperial Army. Now you shall see for yourselves the fate of a *josenpi* who resists us!"

As soon as the monster had finished his speech, he laid his sword on the ground beside him and pulled out a pistol. He pointed it at the woman and fired three shots. The woman's blood splattered all around her, and she lay still.

I suppose that creep did the same thing to her that he did to me. She probably held back until she just couldn't take it anymore. I bet that's when she fought back. I wonder if she bit his hand or broke his finger.

As I watched the woman's final moments, I was tormented by the thought that we had no control over our own lives. That woman's cruel death could easily be mine tomorrow or the next day. Faced with such horror, we all breathlessly tried to hold back our silent tears. A few women began to sob, and their weeping swiftly spread throughout the group. Then the monster fired his gun into the air.

"*Josenpi*! Do you all want to die? Your tears should only be shed for the Imperial Army! You're dismissed!"

We headed back to our rooms, leaving the woman's body behind us. I hated myself for still being alive.

I don't know how much longer I can endure this terrible situation.

I gritted my teeth and clenched my trembling fists.

At the Yangjiazhai comfort station, autumn had passed, and winter was upon us. One Sunday, I received a visitor who acted a little different than usual. When he came through the door, he looked around the room and then at me. Usually, soldiers were on top of me almost as soon as they stepped into the room.

The soldier sat down on the bed and let out a long sigh.

"You're from Korea, aren't you?" he asked.

The moment I heard his words, I felt a blend of happiness and shame, just as when I'd met the man from Tongyeong back in Inner Mongolia.

"I'm from Chungcheong Province," he said.

The words made my heart skip a beat. Though I was happy to see another Korean, I was also afraid he might know who I was. The sad fact was that, even though I wasn't to blame for my current situation, I didn't want anyone to know about it.

When I hesitated, the man from Chungcheong Province

went on. "When I was a kid, I went to Japan with my dad. Later, I was drafted into the Japanese army. My parents live in Japan."

It was only then that I was able to relax.

"To be honest, I didn't want to visit the comfort station," the man said with a sigh. "There are some Japanese soldiers who don't like coming here either. Our units send us here as if they're doing us some huge favor, but what happens here is so barbaric. They bring young Korean girls here and then…"

I wept as I listened to him speak.

"Don't cry. You must miss your home so much. I wish I could go home, too. If only this insane war would end."

"When do you think that will happen?"

"I guess it'll be over someday. I'm with a support unit, so I've been all over the place. Right now, the troops are all being sent to countries in the south."

"What countries are those?"

"There's Burma, the Philippines, Thailand, and so on. There are quite a few countries down there, actually."

"Will we have to go there?"

"Probably so. The Japanese bring comfort women with them wherever they go."

"Are you going there, too?"

The man from Chungcheong Province nodded his head,

without saying a word. It might have been because he was Korean, but he seemed much different from the Japanese warmongers. As I asked him one question after another, time seemed to fly by. Soon enough, an impatient Japanese soldier outside started cursing.

As the man was about to leave, he turned back to me. "Take care of yourself. I'm leaving here tomorrow."

"You take care of yourself, too."

As I watched the man open the door and step outside, I wept again. After that, it was back to the Japanese soldiers, who were waiting like a pack of hungry wolves.

Far Across the Sea

Heading south, 1942

A few days later, Auntie and Uncle suddenly told us to pack our things. The comfort station was soon filled with the commotion of all the women getting their things together.

I pulled Bok-sun aside for a moment. "I heard the Japanese are going to open a new front in the war. Apparently they're going to take us to the south."

"To the south? What's down there?"

"I'm not sure, either. A lot of countries, I guess. But anyway, it's really far from here."

With a sigh, Bok-sun told me to keep that information to myself.

A truck picked us up and drove us to Shanghai's biggest dock, which was lined with enormous ships. If that Korean soldier hadn't told me that the Japanese were moving south,

I would've assumed those ships were there to take us home.

On orders from the Japanese army, Auntie and Uncle led us aboard one of the ships and then took us to the lowest cabin. With four decks, the ship was much bigger than the comfort station we'd been at.

The cabin at the bottom of the ship was packed with women sitting with their luggage. Some of them had their hair neatly braided and were wearing jackets and skirts. Judging from their outfits, it seemed clear they'd been brought there from Korea, just as I had been. The fear and curiosity in their eyes reminded me of how I'd felt when I left Korea. It was gut-wrenching to see those women.

I decided to strike up a conversation with one of them. "So where did you get on the ship?"

"Busan. Where are we right now anyway? Is the textile mill still a long way off?"

The instant the woman mentioned the textile mill, I realized the Japanese troops were still luring women in with that shameless lie. I felt so sorry for these women, who were doomed to the same fate as me.

Bok-sun mentioned that she'd been taken by ship from Busan to Shanghai and then in a Japanese military truck all the way to Nanjing.

"Was the ship you rode in this big, Bok-sun? This is my first time on a ship, but I've never seen one like this!"

"Yeah, it was. It was a huge warship, just like this one. There were soldiers on the upper decks, and the bottom of the ship was full of women."

We spent a day waiting aboard the ship. The next day, the engine roared to life. Someone explained that the engine was especially loud there, on the lowest deck, since we were right above the engine room.

When the guard wasn't watching, Bok-sun whispered into my ear. "We're finally moving."

There was a stir among the women in the cabin. Their eyes darted around nervously as they wondered where we were headed, how long we'd be on the ship, and whether they'd get seasick. The engine made such a frightful din in the cabin that we couldn't get any sleep. The only way to stay sane was to talk to the other passengers.

The woman who was sitting next to me looked very uneasy. When the guard's attention was diverted, I whispered to her. "Where are you from?"

"I'm from Jeolla Province. It seems like I've been on this ship for quite a while. I was told that Japan was pretty close, so why is it taking so long?"

The woman from Jeolla Province was just as I'd been five years ago—completely in the dark.

I told her the truth. "This ship just left Shanghai, in China, and it's heading to the countries in the south."

She shook her head. "That can't be right! I'm supposed to go to Japan for a job. I'm only here because they told me I could earn money in Japan."

"A long time ago, I was tricked into coming here, too. This ship isn't going to Japan."

The woman from Jeolla Province kept shaking her head and began to sniffle.

Bok-sun gave her a gentle pat on the back. "All of us fell for those Japanese lies. We're all stuck here together now."

The woman from Jeolla Province finally broke into tears.

"Try to relax," I told the woman. "When did you leave home?"

"Nearly a month ago. I'm from Hampyeong in Jeolla Province, and I waited several days in Mokpo. It's been about ten days since I got on the ship. A whole lot of people boarded in Mokpo. Where are you from?"

"I'm from Seosan in Chungcheong Province. Five years ago, I thought I was going to a textile mill in Japan, too."

"If the place we're going isn't a textile mill, what kind of place is it?"

I couldn't bring myself to tell the woman that she was going to become a sex slave for the Japanese army. "Tell me how things are in Korea these days. I left a long time ago, and I'm really curious about how things have changed since then. I'm worried about my mom and little brother, too."

"The Japanese government is trying to make us take Japanese names since we're all supposedly part of the same nation. We don't really have a choice, because people are harassed if they don't."

I thought about my Japanese name, Haruko.

Now they're even making people change their names!

The woman from Jeolla Province hadn't forgotten her question. "So where exactly are we going?"

"We're going to the front where the Japanese troops are fighting."

"To the front? What about the textile mill?"

I had no choice but to tell the woman the whole truth. Since she was already aboard the ship, she had no way to escape her fate. But so that she wouldn't give up hope, I also said she might get to work in the hospital

On the ship, they handed out rice balls two times a day. It was barely enough to keep us from starving. Since we were on the bottom deck, it was impossible to tell whether it was daytime or nighttime.

One day, an armed Japanese soldier came into the cabin and told us to go up to the deck and leave our baggage in the cabin. Once on deck, I saw the ocean and the sky above it, along with an island, not far away. After being confined in that cabin at the bottom of the ship for so long, I felt like I could finally breathe again.

The soldiers lowered boats into the water and had some of the passengers climb aboard. The boats dropped them off at the island and then returned to the ship for another load.

We found ourselves on an uninhabited island. The jungle there was so thick that every step inside was a struggle. We weren't told anything about why we'd had to leave the ship or what the Japanese were doing there. After dropping off all the passengers on the shore, the soldiers returned to the ship.

We stayed on the island for two days. For meals, they brought us rice balls from the ship. On the third day, the boats reappeared and took us back to the ship. On deck, the soldiers handed out odd-looking vests, which they called life jackets. One of these, they told us, would keep us afloat in the water.

"Bok-sun, why do you think they're handing out these jackets?"

"They say there are submarines in the water out there."

I'd never heard of life jackets or submarines before.

Every few days, the ship's engines would be turned off and the ship left to drift, for fear of a submarine attack. Each time, the passengers would be taken on boats to a desert island nearby. The islands were so peaceful that I didn't want to go back to the ship. The sunlight glittered on the waves, and the water was so clear you could see all the way to the bottom. If there was a heaven, I thought, this must be it. But as beautiful as the scenery might be, it couldn't hold a candle to my hometown.

Back on the ship, we kept sailing until we reached a huge harbor. Once again, we were told to leave our things on the ship and disembark. As we set foot on solid ground, I wondered what was going on. The buildings there were much taller than those I'd seen in Shanghai, and there were also Westerners with their fair skin and prominent noses. The city was called Hong Kong.

The Japanese troops escorted us to an inn, where we spent several days under guard. Nearby, there was the deafening roar of bombs and rattle of gunfire.

In a few days, the Japanese troops took us back to the ship. Along the streets, I saw flags emblazoned with the Japanese rising sun flapping in the breeze. The Japanese troops cheered about their big victory in Hong Kong.

Back on the ship, we found quite a few strangers in the cabin. They turned out to be comfort women from Hong Kong. They caught us up on the latest news.

In Japan's war in China, it had conquered the territory between Shanghai and Nanjing and had now taken over Hong Kong, too. The bombs we'd heard in Hong Kong had apparently been part of the Japanese attack. Now the Japanese meant to take over the countries to the south, and it had drafted young men, both Japanese and Korean, to fight its battles. Those young men had been deployed so quickly that they were being trained on board their ships. This made me worry about Jin-gyu and Chun-sik.

Our sea voyage was just as unpleasant as before. We had to disembark and then re-embark time and time again as the ship attempted to evade submarines. The beaches where we had to wait were humid and muggy, and at night the mosquitoes were out in force. A mosquito bite would itch for days and swell up as big as a soybean. The Japanese soldiers handed out vials holding some kind of chemicals and told us to rub the stuff on our skin to keep away malaria-carrying mosquitoes. If we caught malaria, they told us, our lives would be in danger. This scared us, and we made sure to apply the mosquito repellant.

Anyone who came down with malaria and started having diarrhea was quarantined in one corner of the cabin. People said that the malaria patients weren't even being fed. There was another rumor that, if anyone died of the disease, their body would be tossed into the ocean.

As our time at sea dragged on, the food supply became the biggest problem. Eventually, we were only getting one rice ball a day. Whenever we were dropped off on a desert island, the most famished of us would wander through the jungle, looking for something to eat. Bok-sun and I ventured into the jungle, too. We picked tender greens we found there and boiled them to fill our bellies.

After a long stay on one of those desert islands, we were finally taken back to the ship. But only a few hours later, a siren began to wail and a voice over the loudspeaker told the passengers to evacuate the cabins. On deck, Japanese soldiers were handing out life jackets and telling everyone to jump into the water. Bok-sun and I hurried to pull on our life jackets. But when I looked down at the churning water below and tried to jump, my feet just wouldn't leave the deck. A soldier had to push us off. As I fell into the water, I squeezed my eyes shut, convinced that my time on earth was up. But when I came to, I was floating. The life jacket had kept me from sinking. All around me in the water, people were bobbing like ducks.

Where is Bok-sun?

We'd definitely fallen into the water together, but I didn't recognize anyone around me. While I was looking around and calling my friend's name, a big spout of water shot into the air, and a powerful whirlpool sucked me under the water. I couldn't breathe. Again and again, I was hurled to the surface and then dragged down again, until I couldn't even tell whether I was alive or dead.

When I finally came to my senses, I was a long way from

the convoy of ships. The ship I'd been on was still afloat, and I could see soldiers running around on the deck.

I could hardly believe I was alive. I had to hurry and find Bok-sun. Since she'd been wearing a life jacket, just like me, I figured she must still be floating. I called out to her wildly. I was running out of energy, and my arms and legs grew sluggish. Then I saw Bok-sun making her way toward me, flailing her arms and legs.

I burst into tears. "Bok-sun, you're alive! I thought you were a goner."

"I thought I'd lost you, too! Let's tie our life jackets to each other. That way we can stay together whether we live or die. I'm so scared!"

I was so exhausted I could no longer move my legs. Bok-sun and I floated in the water and drifted with the waves. I was terrified there would be another explosion in the water. I was shivering with the cold and slipping in and out of consciousness.

I guess I'm going to die out here in the ocean.

The faces of my mom and Chun-sik flashed before my eyes.

"The ship is putting boats into the water. It looks like they're going to pick us up. Hold on a little longer!" Bok-sun shook me to keep my spirits up.

The soldiers were rescuing people from the water. It was

only after we were back aboard the ship that I felt sure we'd survived.

Fortunately, our ship hadn't been hit during the submarine attack. But the ship ahead of us had been sunk by a torpedo, and our ship had rescued some of the survivors. That ship had been carrying a large number of women and Japanese soldiers, too, and many of them had been killed when the ship was torpedoed. That news made my own survival feel all the more miraculous. The surface of the ocean was dotted with shoes and other effects of the dead.

Nearly a year passed on our journey from Shanghai to Hong Kong and then farther to the south. Much of that time was spent letting the ship drift to dodge submarines and ferrying passengers to desert islands and back to the ship. Our final destination, we were told, was near Manila in the Philippines.

Our Daily Struggle

Leyte Island, Philippines, 1943

In Manila, the weather was so hot and humid that I felt sticky all over. Even the clothes I was wearing felt cumbersome. The Japanese soldiers took us to a large building, which I thought might once have been a government office. On our first day there, we weren't given any work to do. We looked out the windows at the Filipinos outside. They were shorter than Koreans, with big, friendly eyes and healthy, dark complexions. I was especially envious of the women who were holding babies.

Will I ever get to be a mother like those women? When it comes down to it, finding a decent husband might be an even bigger challenge.

It was awful to think of what the Japanese soldiers had done to my body.

Early the next morning, Japanese troops were brought

over in military trucks, which gave me a bad feeling. Just as I'd feared, the soldiers had the women stand in several lines. Some of the lines had twenty or thirty women in them, while others had barely ten. I stayed close to Bok-sun, to make sure we stayed together. The soldiers told us that the groups were being sent to places like Manila, Singapore, and Rangoon, as well as islands I'd never heard of before.

There were ten other women riding on the truck with Bok-sun and me. The truck left downtown Manila and drove for two days straight, making me so carsick I could barely move. This being my first time in the tropics, even the sun up in the sky looked strange, and my home felt even farther away.

After reaching a port in the remote countryside, we spent the night in some kind of warehouse, minus the walls, and boarded a cargo ship the next day. On the ship, I was weighed down by a strange lethargy that made me feel like a stranger looking down at my own body.

After a day and a half on the ship, we arrived at another island, south of the island that Manila was on. Once more, we were loaded into trucks like so much luggage. As we drove along a coastal road, we passed by houses that looked more like huts. Men in loincloths gawked at us with curiosity, as if they'd stumbled upon a fascinating sight.

The truck turned onto a narrow road that cut through

the heavy jungle. The trees were so thick we couldn't even see the sky.

We continued for some time in the shade of the trees. Emerging from the jungle, we saw more of the huts. The truck stopped in front of one of the bigger ones. A middle-aged man and woman stepped out of the building and came up to the truck.

The couple were Japanese, which meant we'd been brought to yet another comfort station. As usual, the couple had us call them Auntie and Uncle. Auntie took a roster of names from a Japanese soldier and assigned our rooms. The roof and even the walls of the huts were made of woven palm leaves. Sure enough, there was a bed and a bucket of water in my room, along with a few bamboo pegs on the wall for hanging up clothing.

"Bok-sun, we're at another one of *those* places."

Bok-sun sighed. As I set down my bundle of clothing in a corner of the room, I felt the energy drain right out of me.

I've got to get out of this sickening lifestyle someday.

The thought that I was even farther away from home now weighed on my chest and made it hard to breathe.

In the evening, a military truck rolled out of the jungle. A short Filipino man climbed off the truck and unloaded a big barrel full of rice. All the women came out of the hut and sat down in the yard to eat. I was used to sticky rice, but this rice was so airy that a good puff would send it flying. Even so, I was glad to see rice. I scrunched the fluffy rice into balls and stuffed them into my mouth. The rice's rough texture wasn't very appetizing, but what was even worse was the thought that I'd have to keep eating food like this to survive in this foreign country.

Bok-sun and I must have been thinking the same thing, because when our eyes met, both of us broke into tears. All at once, the sky turned as gloomy as our thoughts had been. There was a sharp crack of thunder, followed by a torrential downpour. Soon, the ditches were overflowing. The rain fell in great sheets but was too warm to feel very refreshing. As soon as the torrent was over, the clouds opened up and revealed blazing sunshine. The weather in that country was fickle.

Over the past few years, my life has been an unending series of horrors. Will the sunlight shine down on me someday? I wonder what the Japanese soldiers here are like.

The first night at the new comfort station gave a taste of the mugginess we'd have to endure.

Breakfast the next day was served at the comfort station. As soon as the meal was over, Auntie and Uncle called us over. There was a truck waiting outside.

The truck drove farther and farther down a narrow track that ran through the jungle. We kept going until we reached a hospital, which was quite large given its location deep in the jungle. By its entrance, there was a wide road for big trucks. I figured there were a large number of Japanese units nearby.

The hospital had two stories, and on the first story, there were many wounded Japanese soldiers lying on the bare floor. There were soldiers with bandages on their head or arms, as well as amputees, missing an arm or a leg. Some of the injured soldiers begged us to help them. I didn't see any nurses around.

I wish they'd have us take care of the injured soldiers instead of what we're doing!

With an involuntary shudder, I was reminded of the wounded soldier who'd tried to rape Bok-sun. I hated all Japanese soldiers. Even so, I was willing to do anything that wasn't comfort woman work.

Auntie took us to the second floor of the hospital, where we were tested for venereal diseases. We lay down on a wooden bed and spread our legs while the doctor poked around with a device that looked like a duck's beak, checking for infection. Women who were infected with syphilis had to take a shot called "Number 606." This shot produced a hideous stench in the mouth and nose that ruined people's appetite. As a comfort woman, I wasn't sure whether it was better to come down with a disease or to stay disease-free.

Part of me wanted to get sick so I could take a break from our awful routine, but another part of me thought it was more important to stay healthy.

The flow of soldiers resumed the next day. Women with a venereal disease or a bad inflammation were given a few days' break from their duties. Most of the soldiers we were servicing were from the ground forces, and I was astounded by how many soldiers passed through the comfort station.

The young Filipino who'd brought our rice on the first day came by every few days with groceries and condoms. He told us that all our supplies came from the field hospital.

As Uncle handed out the condoms, he told us there was such a rush of soldiers that we'd have to wash the condoms and reuse them. Every time I washed used condoms, I felt sick. They were an important tool, since they kept us from catching venereal diseases and also from getting pregnant. But there were a lot of soldiers who wanted to have sex without wearing a condom. When we told the soldiers they had to wear one anyway, some of them would beat us. There was no one we could complain to about a beating.

Sometimes, one of the women would get pregnant, but I never saw any of them actually give birth. Some pregnant women had to service so many soldiers that they died from blood loss.

Bok-sun and I would briefly meet while we were doing

the laundry or washing the condoms. It's scary to think what people are capable of getting used to. The first day I washed the condoms, it was so awful and disgusting that I cried and threw up. But after a while, I became desensitized to it. When I imagined that the condoms were Japanese soldiers, I sometimes even got a little pleasure out of smacking, squeezing, and pummeling them. The only thing that got me through each day was the vague hope that someday I'd get to take revenge on the Japanese soldiers. And when we took our weekly trip to the hospital, I'd pretend we were going on an outing.

There were no differences between the seasons on the island: the weather was muggy in spring, summer, fall, and winter. Maybe that's why I longed so much for the spring breezes of my home and for the spreading oak tree that overlooked the pass at Hakdoljae. I had visions of cosmos flowers swaying in the autumn fields, and I dearly missed Mt. Dobisan's snow-covered peak. Once my thoughts turned to my mom and little brother, my longing turned into tears. Despite the weeping such longing always invoked, it also gave me the strength to endure those terrible days.

The young Filipino who ran errands between the comfort station and the hospital was named Liam. He had big eyes and a dusky face, and when he smiled, his eyes seemed to hold wells of secret longing. Seeing Liam made me think of Chun-sik. When our eyes met, I couldn't help smiling, too. Perhaps because of my fondness for Liam, he took special care of me. On some days, he'd bring me a mango without telling the others; on other days, he'd bring over chili peppers because he'd heard that Koreans like spicy food.

Liam spoke good Japanese, and whenever he saw me, he'd tell me he didn't like Japan and that we should hang on a little longer, since the war would be over soon. He was a cool breeze that brought some relief from my distress. Through Liam, we learned that the island we were on was called Leyte and that American troops had landed there. When Liam told us the war was ending, Bok-sun and I asked him what we should do after that. Liam said he supported the United States and told us the Americans would help us.

But Auntie and Uncle told us a different story. They said the American troops were even worse than the Japanese troops and that they desperately hoped the United States wouldn't win the war. We weren't sure whom to believe. The only thing we wanted was to go back home.

One day, a soldier came into my room who looked younger than usual. Most Japanese soldiers wasted no time in pulling their pants down, but this one was different. He seemed like he wanted to talk to me, but he hesitated, like a bashful schoolboy.

"Listen, I'm a student who was drafted to fight in this war. You're from Korea, right?"

"Yeah, I am," I replied. This teenage boy reminded me of Chun-sik.

"My family is from Seonsan in Gyeongsang Province. How did you end up at...?" The young soldier, who was gazing at me with pity in his eyes, couldn't bring himself to finish his sentence.

I told him how I'd been tricked by the Japanese, taken all the way to Inner Mongolia, and then brought here.

"This war will be over soon. Japan is losing," the young soldier said. That was exactly what Liam had told me.

"No kidding? Does that mean we'll get to go home, too?"

"I would think so. There's a rumor going around that the American army is going to launch a big counteroffensive soon."

"If the Americans win, what happens to us?"

"Since the Japanese army brought you here, obviously they'll have to send you back home. You won't have to wait much longer. The Japanese supply lines are under attack. They won't be able to hold out for long."

The young soldier just sat there and chatted with me, without even taking his clothes off. When the Japanese soldiers outside yelled at him to hurry up, he told me to take care of myself and left the room.

Every once in a while, I found myself wondering about that young soldier. He'd said the war was almost over, but we didn't see any changes in our routine. A few months later, the young soldier came back.

"What happened to you? I've been really worried about you."

"I was selected for the special forces and sent to an island where an airfield was being built. But our supply line was cut, and I nearly starved to death."

"I'm just glad you made it back alive."

With a shudder, the soldier went on. "The Japanese soldiers killed all the workers they brought over from Korea. We buried the workers while the soldiers weren't watching. I felt so sorry for them, you know? There were also comfort women on that island…"

"What happened to the comfort women?"

The soldier seemed to be in a daze. "They killed all the comfort women, too. Then they stacked up their corpses, poured kerosene on them, and set them on fire. The Japanese have gone crazy. They're in panic mode since they're being pushed back by the Americans on every front."

The young soldier took some money out of his pocket. "Take this and use it when you get home someday."

"Why are you giving this to me?"

The young soldier shook his head. "There's no chance I'll make it back alive. The Japanese are using students like me as cannon fodder. They sent us here today one last time, as if it were some special reward. But I don't want to commit any more sins. That's why I've brought you all my money. Please don't refuse my gift."

As I listened to the young soldier, my eyes filled with tears. I could sense the sincerity in his words. I was moved by how kindly he was treating me with death looming before him.

"I can't take this money. You have to go back home, too."

The young soldier shook his head. "There's no way for us to survive. Koreans are just expendable targets. I saw it with my own eyes. And so…"

The young soldier's words broke off, and he began to weep. I wept with him. After he left, the next Japanese soldier came in, but my mind was elsewhere.

That evening, I got a clandestine visit from Liam. He didn't waste any time in small talk. "You've got to get out of here. I've heard that the Americans are going to launch a full-scale attack on this island soon."

Liam's words got my attention.

Late that night, after all the soldiers had returned to their units, I passed Liam's message along to Bok-sun.

"Are you serious? Did he say he'd help us escape?"

"All he said is that we should escape together. I still don't know what we're supposed to do."

Bok-sun mulled it over for a while and then slowly shook her head. "Chun-ja, if we run away from here, where would we go? And how would we get home, when we sailed thousands of miles to get here in the first place? The war is supposed to be over soon, so we should just wait it out."

"If we didn't have to do this awful job anymore, would it really matter where we went?"

"No, we should just be patient and stay out of trouble until the war is over. The Japanese brought us here, and they'll take us back again. That's our only way home."

Bok-sun took my hands in hers and begged me not to do anything rash. And then she lifted up her top and showed me her bare skin. I was shocked to see a horrific burn mark running down the center of her chest.

"What's that, Bok-sun? What happened to you?"

"I ran away once, early on. When they caught me, they seared me here with a red-hot iron. I thought I was going to die."

Hearing her story made me weep.

"Even back then, they treated me cruelly when I got caught trying to escape. Nowadays, they'd have killed me without a second thought. You know how cold-blooded and merciless the Japanese are. And right now, they're desperate, too."

"You're right, Bok-sun. There were some Korean women like us on an island where an airfield was being built, and they were all killed when the Japanese retreated. There's really no telling what those Japanese are going to do."

"That's why I'm saying we shouldn't be in a hurry to run off, because we might get caught."

While I'd been excited by Liam's advice, seeing the scar on Bok-sun's chest made me think again.

The very next day, I heard a scream from Bok-sun's room, followed by a heavy thud and a Japanese soldier cursing.

As soon as the Japanese soldier in my room was gone, I ran over to Bok-sun's room. When I was about to open the door, it burst open and a Japanese soldier with a beet-red face came charging out.

"Get out of my way, stupid girl!" he screamed.

I cowered away in fear. Auntie ran over in her clogs. Bok-sun's room reeked of blood. Bok-sun herself was lying on the floor, blood gushing from her thigh. Auntie wrapped a piece of cloth around her thigh and tied it off.

"What happened, Bok-sun?" I asked.

My friend's face was growing paler. "My thigh… with a pocketknife…"

"What got into you?" Auntie grumbled reproachfully.

"You're supposed to be accommodating. What have I always told you? Don't get on the soldiers' nerves! That's how you stay alive."

Her forehead creasing, Bok-sun struggled to speak. "He told me to lie face down. When I said I couldn't do that because it hurts too much, he lunged at me with his knife and said he was going to kill me."

Even though I hadn't been in the room with Bok-sun, I could well imagine what had happened. One of the items the Japanese soldiers carried around with them was a multi-tool knife with a nail clipper and several small blades. I'd been threatened by that knife a time or two myself.

Bok-sun had lost so much blood that she was anemic for a while. There was no way to get a blood transfusion in a war zone, and no one would've been willing to donate blood to a comfort woman anyway. Auntie was upset with Bok-sun for not being able to service any soldiers and complained about how long it was taking her to heal.

The attack left Bok-sun extremely weak, and she sometimes raved in apparent delirium.

I asked Liam to bring some food that would help with Bok-sun's anemia.

"She needs to eat some meat, but that's not easy to come by. Just make sure she has plenty of rice." Liam felt so bad for Bok-sun that he sneaked a hard-boiled egg into the comfort station.

"Bok-sun, Liam says you need to eat a lot. Here's an egg he brought just for you."

Bok-sun managed to open her eyes and eat the hard-boiled egg. Auntie didn't pay any attention to Bok-sun's health—her only apparent concern was when Bok-sun could start servicing Japanese soldiers again. The lives of the comfort women were always cheap. Without letting Auntie know, I kept Bok-sun supplied with the food that Liam brought for her.

"Thank you, Chun-ja."

I hushed her. "Keep your voice down. If Auntie finds out, she'll make a scene."

When no one was watching, I'd head over to Bok-sun's room and take care of her. My nursing seemed to make a difference, because color returned to her ashen face and her injury began to heal.

"Chun-ja, I'm afraid of getting better. That means going back to our awful job. I'd rather just stay sick like this."

"Don't talk like that, Bok-sun! You don't actually think Auntie would put up with that, do you? I know how you feel, but you've got to get better. What if the wound doesn't heal and festers instead?"

When a comfort woman got sick, the Japanese would

stop feeding them or just leave them to die. Without me taking care of her, Bok-sun's condition would have gotten worse, which could've led to her death. But within a week, she was back on her feet.

When Auntie saw Bok-sun on her way to the cafeteria, she gave the sick woman a sidelong look. "She's a fighter, that's for sure! But she ought to be pulling her load as a *jo-senpi*, especially at such a crucial time as this."

Auntie's grumbling made anger blaze up inside me, but I managed to make a civil response, for Bok-sun's sake.

"Don't worry, Auntie. I'm going to help her make a quick recovery."

"That's right. The sooner Fumiko gets back to servicing the men, the sooner we can lighten your load."

To be honest, I was willing to take on Bok-sun's whole quota of soldiers if I thought it would help her. But it was a relief to know that Auntie wouldn't interfere with me taking care of Bok-sun.

"When Auntie thought you were going to die, she wouldn't let anyone visit you. But now that you seem to be getting better, she's already scheming to put you back to work. I guess our lives really don't mean a thing to them. That's why we have to do whatever it takes to survive. Keep your strength up, Bok-sun, OK?"

Bok-sun squeezed my hand in gratitude.

Within a few days, Auntie started letting Japanese soldiers visit Bok-sun's room again.

An Unblessed Baby

Field hospital, 1944

As time went by, more and more Japanese soldiers came through the comfort station. On some days, more than forty visited my room. I wasn't a person, but a mere tool for satisfying the soldiers' animalistic lust. After every horrible visit, I knew that I was supposed to dilute the disinfectant and rinse my private parts with it, but sometimes I was just too exhausted.

I would sometimes pass out and not wake up until a whole troop of soldiers had come and gone. What scared me the most was the soldiers who refused to wear a condom. Most of the soldiers would put one on without my asking, but I had to argue with some of the younger soldiers about it.

The younger the soldier, the more they behaved like a wild animal.

Whenever a soldier rushed at me, I'd hold out a condom and insist they wear it.

One day, a young-looking soldier was particularly stubborn.

"When I go to the battle tomorrow, I'm going to be killed. This is the last day of my life! I want to leave a child behind me. I don't want to die like this!"

With a sob, the young soldier threw himself on me. The condom was the only thing I had to protect my body. In desperation, I tried to push him off me, but I was too weak to resist his youthful lust. Like a madman, he beat me and came at me again. In the end, I fainted. When I finally came to myself, the soldier was pulling up his pants with a pathetic grin on his face. Struggling to my feet, I mixed the disinfectant in water and splashed it on my private parts. I rinsed again and again until I wanted to puke.

That day, there seemed to be no end of such beasts. They all said they were about to die, that this was their last visit to the comfort station, and that they were going to be cannon fodder. They sounded like a recorded message that was playing on repeat.

Late that night, I went to see Bok-sun.

"I had a lot of weird soldiers today," I told her.

Bok-sun nodded her head in agreement. "Same here. There were a lot of new recruits, and nearly all of them were crying and throwing a fit. This is all so horrible. I wish I could just die, I really do. One of the soldiers gave me his belongings before leaving. He gave me a photo of his kid and said he was going to die the next day. Take a look at this."

Bok-sun showed me a photograph of a baby, so worn-out that it was about to fall apart. There was also an envelope with some money in it.

"What's all this?"

"The soldier told me this is a photograph of his son on his first birthday and cried because he won't get to see him again. This is his address. He wants me to send the photograph and money there if I ever make it back alive."

"Bok-sun, it looks like the war really is coming to an end. What are we supposed to do when Japan is defeated?"

"That soldier told me that the Japanese army's line of supply has been cut off by the American offensive. So the Japanese are hurrying to escape and only leaving behind enough soldiers to slow the Americans down. He said this was his last visit to the comfort station before his death. You know, I kind of feel sorry for these young soldiers. It's their country that I hate for starting the war."

Bok-sun stuck the baby photograph and the envelope into her bundle of things.

Why do people go to war? Every war comes to an end

someday, and for every winner, there's a loser. The loser dreams of revenge, which eventually leads to another war. Why was it our fate to be dragged off to take part in another country's war and to suffer such horrible things every day?

The Japanese army seemed to regard these trips to the comfort station as one final reward for the young soldiers who were being expended to buy the rest of the army time to get away. That attitude disgusted me.

During the visits by these doomed soldiers, who were facing war with all its horror, I felt sorry for them. I couldn't help wondering what cruel fate had doomed me and them to suffer like this in a foreign land. Since every soldier who came to the comfort station said the war was almost over, I couldn't help wondering where this endless procession of soldiers was coming from. Every last one of them was young, short, and scrawny.

One day, I got a visit from a boy who looked too skinny to be a soldier.

As soon as he came in, he fell on my knees, as if it were his mother's lap, and wept, his shoulders heaving. I pitied the boy, and as I watched him crying harder and harder, tears came to my eyes, too.

"I'm sorry. Seeing you makes me think of my mom, and my big sister, too. Tomorrow, I have to fly a plane into the battle. I'm a kamikaze pilot, so I can't come back alive. But I don't want to die."

The boy started crying even harder.

"What's a kamikaze pilot?" I asked.

The boy looked up at me, his eyes brimming over with tears. He had the eyes of a lost puppy, looking for its mother.

"It means I'm a suicide pilot. They forced me to swear the oath. They say I have to die honorably for the emperor. They say that's the only way my family can keep its honor. There are many boys like me who've had to make that oath."

I asked the frail-looking boy why he'd become a soldier.

"Kamikaze pilots like me have to be lightweight. My officers told me that I'm perfect for this holy war and that my body will bring glory to the emperor. All I wanted to do was fly planes, but they pushed me to become a kamikaze, to be a hero in our holy war. But my plane and I will be smashed to pieces. I really don't want to die."

The boy's story touched my heart. "Are you going to fly the plane into battle?"

"Tomorrow, they're going to have me fly toward an American warship. They won't put enough gas in the plane for me to come back. My plane and I will crash into the ship. The plane, the ship, and my body will all be blown to bits. I'm so scared!"

Listening to the boy was enough to give me the shivers. As death approached, he wanted to receive comfort from me in the purest sense of the word. I wrapped him in my arms.

As I held the boy, he sang to himself in a low voice.

My heart sets out,

An airplane in the blue sky.

The engine hums as I turn the wheel.

Mother, I have to leave you behind.

When you get my ashes, embrace them as you would me.

I found it harder and harder to understand how Japan could send such sweet young boys into the jaws of death.

Who are they fighting this war for?

The Japanese were lunatics, slaughtering their own people and dragging off young girls from a neighboring country into a life of slavery and abuse. This boy soldier was a victim of this unhappy age, just like me. I sincerely comforted him, and after a long cry on my lap, he thanked me and left the room.

As he walked away, I wished him a safe return from the bottom of my heart. "I hope you survive and see your parents again."

Afterward, I felt a heaviness in my chest and had trouble getting to sleep. Whenever I thought of the boy, I would get bloated, as if I had indigestion, and I sometimes had bouts of dry heaving.

At mealtime one day, the very smell of rice made me

retch.

"Chun-ja, is your stomach upset? Did you get food poisoning?" Bok-sun said, staring at me with concern.

"I'm not really sure. Thinking of that boy soldier makes me worried that Chun-sik got drafted, too. Why can't I stop thinking of that boy?"

"When it comes down to it, we're the bigger victims. That boy gets to die for his own country, so why should we pity him? You must have some pretty bad indigestion. I'll go get some medicine from Auntie."

But even after I took the medicine Bok-sun brought me, the nausea didn't go away. Over time, the retching got worse.

Late one night, Bok-sun sneaked into my room. "You're not pregnant, are you?"

The question took me by surprise. But upon reflection, it did seem like I'd missed a period.

"Now that you mention it, my cycle has been a little off."

"Think carefully. Have you missed the date or not?"

I counted the days on my fingers. "It's probably nothing. Maybe my period is a little late because I've been sick. It's pretty common for me to skip a month or two."

All at once, I was reminded of the day I'd had my first period, four years after being taken to Inner Mongolia. At the time, I thought I'd come down with some terrible disease.

Bok-sun looked worried. "Didn't you tell them to use a condom?"

"The soldiers have been acting really strange lately. Some of them jumped right on top of me without wearing a condom. I tried to resist, but I just wasn't strong enough to stop them. Bok-sun, what if I'm actually having a baby?"

"Give it some time. After all, you might not be pregnant. Whatever happens, you always have to be careful."

"It has been a while since my last period, but that's happened before."

"Have you had dry heaves before?"

I shook my head as fear swept over me.

"When I was in Nanjing," Bok-sun said, "one of the women there was just like you. She kept retching and couldn't bear the smell of food. Oh, I really hope this turns out to be nothing."

"What if I do end up being pregnant? I don't want to have a baby with Japanese blood, but it would be my first child."

The more I thought about it, the more nervous I felt. It was driving me crazy.

"Do you think I should tell Auntie?"

"You can't tell her right now. If the Japanese think you're pregnant, they'll do something nasty to you. When the woman I knew in Nanjing started showing, they took her away, and we never saw her again."

"Where did they take her? Are you sure they didn't let her have the baby?"

Bok-sun nodded her head sadly.

The Japanese soldiers cared little about whether the comfort women lived or died. They weren't about to take care of a woman who got pregnant in the war or keep her safe until she gave birth.

From then on, Bok-sun and I waited to eat until everyone else was done to avoid attracting attention. When I was by myself, I tried punching myself in the belly, jumping from my bed onto the floor, and holding my breath as long as I could. But that just wore me out and made me weaker. Every day, I waited for a period that never came. Every time I went to the bathroom, I fretfully looked for a change that never occurred.

The time had come to visit the hospital again, our first visit in quite a while. When we'd first arrived at this comfort station, we were taken to the field hospital once a week for testing and treatment. But after the soldiers started flooding into the comfort station, our hospital visits were cut to once every other week, and now nearly two months had gone by since our last visit. Hoping I could skip the checkup, I stayed in bed, pretending to be sick.

When Auntie shouted at me to hurry up, Bok-sun came

to get me.

"Bok-sun, I'm too scared to go. What happens if I'm really pregnant?"

"Not going might look even more suspicious. I don't know what to tell you. I had a few soldiers who didn't wear condoms, but my period started yesterday. What a relief—I was so anxious!"

"Bok-sun, I can't go to the hospital. Can you tell Auntie I'm too sick to get up? I'm scared to death."

While the rest of the comfort women were at the hospital, my mind was racing. I didn't have the slightest desire to have a child, let alone one fathered by those terrible Japanese soldiers. I felt queasy and kept retching even though I hadn't eaten anything.

After the women returned, Auntie came by to check on me. I came up with a fib—I'd been really sick earlier but felt a little better now. Auntie told me there was no getting out of the next checkup. At mealtime, I brought the food back to my room and forced myself to eat it. My body had become as skinny as a bamboo skewer. Bok-sun said I was definitely pregnant.

A month later, Auntie seemed to have gotten wind of my condition. This time, she made sure I was the first person in the truck. The fateful moment was approaching.

If I turn out to be pregnant, what's going to happen to me?

They wouldn't kill me, would they? Would they make me get an abortion right away?

I was so scared. While the truck was driving down the jungle road, I felt the urge to jump off. But the jungle was a dangerous place, and I knew that if I did jump, I'd be shot before I even hit the ground.

After arriving at the hospital, I waited in line, my heart fluttering inside my chest. Finally, it was my turn. I twitched anxiously. The army doctor looked me over for a long time. The checkup seemed to take twice as long as usual.

After the checkup, Auntie called me over. "Why didn't you use a condom? They say you've been pregnant for quite some time!"

With a sinking feeling, all the horrible stories I'd heard came back to mind. I was terrified that the Japanese would whisk me off to be killed. I was sure they wouldn't let me carry the baby to term.

Auntie gave me a disapproving look. "Do you think those condoms are party favors? What a dumb *josenpi*!"

"I told you the soldiers were a bunch of maniacs and didn't give me a choice! What am I supposed to do now?"

"What do you mean, 'what am I supposed to do?'" Auntie gave me a pack of pills. "Starting today, take this medicine before meals. You've got to get rid of this baby before it grows any bigger! This is a crucial time, the final stage of our holy war. This is when you *josenpi* ought to be doing your best to keep up the morale of the Imperial Army!"

Auntie's words set my teeth on edge.

She calls this a holy war? Who is this holy war being fought for? What's so holy about a war where they kidnap women from a foreign country to be their sex slaves and then, as if that weren't bad enough, force their own countrymen to become suicide pilots? Why should Korean girls have to "comfort" Japanese soldiers who've been drafted to fight for these lunatics?

It was mind-boggling to think there was new life growing inside me, the child of an unknown father. The fact that life had been conceived in my brutalized body should have been a cause for joy. But I was increasingly horrified by the thought that the child inside me had been fathered by a Japanese soldier. I shook my head. That seed should never have taken root there, and I couldn't let it grow. I couldn't let another bear my sad fate. Not being able to take joy in my first child pained me to the core. I couldn't go back to my mom and younger brother carrying the child of a despicable Japanese soldier.

As I held one of the pills that Auntie had given me, I spoke to the child inside me.

I'm sorry. I'm really sorry.

I sobbed, tears pouring from my eyes. By pure force of

will, I put the pill into my mouth. I took another pill the next day, and then the day after that, while telling my baby I was sorry and asking for forgiveness. But the days went by without any change. My dry heaving was getting worse, and I was losing weight, since I could hardly eat anything. Each passing day made me more and more afraid. I'd wanted time to fly by before, but now I wanted it to stop, out of fear that the baby would get bigger and my stomach start to show.

When I fell asleep, frightening dreams passed before my eyes. Sometimes I dreamed that a monster came out of my belly and strangled me. Even in the dream, I couldn't see its features.

Please forgive me!

After ten days passed without any physical effect, Auntie gave me what she said was a stronger medicine and told me to take it twice a day. All it did was make my heart palpitate. The only person I could be honest with was Bok-sun.

"Since the drugs I'm taking are so strong, I suppose the baby wouldn't be normal even if they did let me give birth. Isn't there something I can do, Bok-sun?"

But Bok-sun just shook her head and let out a long sigh.

At last she said, "I heard there's a pregnant woman in the other hut, too. While I was eating earlier, someone was saying that Uncle lost his temper with her."

"How come?"

"He was screaming about 'these stupid *josenpi*.' I guess he was talking about you and that woman. They're taking her to the hospital tomorrow, so I guess they'll take you, too."

That scared me even more.

What are they going to do to me at the hospital? I guess they'll give me an abortion. What did I do to deserve this?

That night, I wasn't able to sleep at all. Throughout the night, I was racked with guilt for the baby in my womb, who for all I knew might be suffering as much as me.

At daybreak the next day, Uncle came to get me. Going outside, I saw a younger-looking woman standing next to Uncle. Soon enough, a truck pulled up. Bok-sun came out to watch me get in the truck, a worried look on her face.

When we arrived at the hospital, Uncle took us to a different room from the one where we had our usual check-ups. There was a large light fixture on the ceiling and several machines in the room that I'd never seen before. The army doctor came in. Uncle held up two fingers, which I took to mean the two of us.

When Uncle left the room, shutting the door behind him, I felt a spike of fear. The doctor told me to lie down on the bed. When I hesitated, his tone grew harsher.

"Stop dawdling and lie down on the bed!"

"What are you going to do to me?"

"Shut your mouth and lie down," he shouted. "I'm in a hurry here."

I assumed they were going to abort my baby, but I'd wanted to know for sure. Rough hands seized me and dragged me toward the bed. Filled with fear, I tossed my head.

The army doctor shoved me down onto the bed and stuck a needle into my arm. My vision dimmed, and my consciousness faded. Vaguely, I wondered if I was going to die. After that, I didn't feel anything.

I was awoken by pain and a shudder running through my body.

How long have I been out?

It felt as if my abdomen was being gouged out. My hands were strapped to the bed railing. The pain was so bad I couldn't help moaning for my mom. I tried to scream, but that only made the splitting pain in my abdomen worse. There was a bandage wrapped around my belly. It seemed clear that they'd cut open my belly to remove the baby.

Was that really necessary?

I wanted to cry with the sorrow and horror of it all. But my abdomen was so sore I couldn't even take a deep breath, let alone cry.

"What did you do to my belly? What happened to the baby?"

"Baby? What baby?" the doctor barked. "The bloody mess that was in there is gone now!"

That ill-fated baby wasn't inside me anymore. Even though the father had been a Japanese soldier, it hurt me to think that the first life conceived in my body had been snuffed out.

Who's to blame for all my misfortune?

Because of my harsh fate, my unblessed baby was gone forever, without a chance to see the world outside. But I couldn't feel either sorrow or joy. It hurt to breathe, it hurt to cough, and it felt like my abdomen would split open at the slightest motion.

Five days after the operation, I was sent back to the comfort station. The woman who'd accompanied me to the hospital said she'd been given an abortion, too

I was given a break from servicing soldiers until my stitches were removed.

When this awful time of my life is over, I hope I'm able to have another baby. I wonder if the one I was carrying was a boy or a girl.

Even though I hadn't wanted that baby, I hated the fact that its life had been taken against my will. Every night, I was tormented by bizarre nightmares. In some of them, my mother called my name and then shook her fist at me when I approached. In others, a baby with an unseen face crawled toward me on the street. I would wake up with a start, drenched in sweat. When night fell, I was afraid of having another horrific dream.

After two weeks, I was taken to the field hospital to get my stitches removed. When they took off the bandages, I got to see my stomach for the first time. Below my belly button was a hideous gash that had been sewn together. The scar ran down my belly like a centipede. It wasn't the kind of scar that would fade over time. Disturbed by the aftermath of the operation, not to mention the soldiers' constant abuse, I wept. I missed my mom desperately.

I had to start servicing soldiers again the day after my stitches were removed. I was determined not to accept any soldiers unless they wore a condom. I didn't want to go through all that pain again.

Weirdly enough, three or four months passed after the operation without a period. For the first month or two, I just assumed it was because my body was still weak from the operation. If I were pregnant, I'd be feeling queasy, but I still had a strong appetite and wasn't bothered by the smell of food. Whenever I relieved myself without seeing any sign of a period, I worried that I might be pregnant again.

Nearly half a year went by like that. I kept my lack of a period to myself at first but then finally mentioned it to Bok-sun. The news took her by surprise.

"I wonder if you—" Bok-sun said and then stopped, shaking her head forcefully. "No, surely not. They couldn't have done that to you!"

"What are you talking about?"

Bok-sun took my hands in a calming gesture and chose her words carefully. "I'm just worried they might have taken out your womb along with the baby. If you haven't had a single period since then… I really hope they didn't do that. But ask Auntie about it. She'll know."

I was having trouble processing this. "What do you mean, they might have taken out my womb? Would that keep me from having a period?"

Bok-sun nodded weakly. My body went limp, and I fell to the floor. I didn't want to believe it.

Are human beings capable of such wickedness?

It was inconceivable. I shook my head.

My body is probably just worn out because of that big surgery.

I shook my head more firmly, convinced that Bok-sun must be wrong.

The womb is the uterus. If they removed my uterus, that means I couldn't ever have a baby.

If Bok-sun was right, I wanted my life to be over. If they'd taken away not only my baby but also my womb, there could be no forgiveness for their sin.

"Bok-sun, surely nobody could be so cruel!" I said, pressing my friend to answer.

"I wish I felt the same way. But I've heard about that kind of thing happening before. I've heard about pregnant women having their wombs ripped out because they were getting in the way of the women's duty to comfort the Imperial Army. Only terrible people could commit such unspeakable acts. I hope that's not what happened to you, I really do!"

But Bok-sun looked uneasy. I was sure she was wrong, but I was fearful all the same.

Day after day, I waited for my period to start. But the more time that passed, the more I thought that Bok-sun might be right after all. Finally, I worked up the courage to check with Auntie. She nonchalantly told me I should be glad I didn't have to worry about getting pregnant anymore.

In that moment, my world seemed to turn upside down and inside out.

I had no more reason to go on. I couldn't stop crying at the thought of it. That night, after the soldiers had gone, I opened my sewing box and took out a pair of scissors.

On top of being raped, now I can't even bear children. I can't face my mom like this!

Every hope I'd had was gone. I had no more reason to live. I didn't want to be raped anymore.

Going on like this would be a living hell.

I made up my mind to die and begged my mom to forgive me. I climbed onto my bed and lay down, facing the ceiling. I held the scissor blade against my wrist. In a life without hope, the only choice was death.

I need to cut the vein on my first try…

I shut my eyes and breathed in deep: three, two, one. I pulled the scissors blade again my wrist as hard as I could. The dull, rusty blade tore through the top layer of the skin and drew blood, but it didn't go very deep. With my eyes still closed, I bit my lips and cut my wrist several more times, but I couldn't reach the vein. The ball of grief inside me exploded, bringing tears to my eyes. I sobbed on and on until the sound brought Bok-sun, in the next room, running to see me.

"Chun-ja! Don't do this. Oh, Chun-ja!"

Bok-sun grabbed the scissors and flung them to the floor and then took me in her arms.

"Death won't fix anything. Remember how you told me we have to do whatever it takes to stay alive? You can't give up! We have to keep going. OK, Chun-ja?"

By this point, Bok-sun was crying, too. It took me a while to pull myself together and grit my teeth once more.

I'm going to make it back alive. I'm going to make them pay someday. If I die now, all the awful things I've suffered won't mean anything. I'm going to stay alive and let the whole world know the terrible things the Japanese army did to us.

Run Away with Me

Jungle, 1945

All of a sudden, an airplane roared overhead. There was a flash of light from the plane, and then several more. After each flash, there was an explosion somewhere in the jungle. One of the bombs blew up close at hand with a shattering boom that seemed to send the whole world topsy-turvy. The women in the comfort station all ran out of their rooms in confusion.

"I guess the war is about to end!"

"What do we do now?"

As we were getting our things together, Auntie and Uncle showed up and yelled at us to get back in our rooms and stay there until we got orders from the Japanese army.

Over the past few days, we'd often heard the roar of artillery nearby. On the day the airplane flew by, we hadn't even had anything to eat because Liam hadn't been able to make his supply run. He didn't show up at the comfort station until nearly lunchtime the next day.

When Uncle complained about how long it had taken Liam to get there, Liam lost his cool. "The field hospital is a complete mess right now. Like I said, the Americans have launched their final attack. The lines of supply are all cut. The only reason I even brought supplies today is because I felt bad for you."

I felt grateful to Liam for going to such risk to bring the supplies. That evening, Liam slipped into my room and brought me some fruit.

Liam spoke quickly. "If you want to survive, you've got to get out of here. You need to run away with me tomorrow. Get your stuff ready and wait for my signal. If you stay here, you're all going to die."

As I listened to Liam, my chest tightened with anxiety.

"Before long, the American army is going to attack the whole island. If you run away with me, you can wait until the Americans arrive and let them arrange your trip home. All the higher-ups at the field hospital have already fled. Some of the Japanese soldiers have jumped off cliffs, and others have committed hara-kiri. If you want to make it out of here, you've got to listen to me."

I didn't know what to say to Liam. Once again, he said we probably wouldn't survive if we didn't do as he said. My heart was pounding with fear, and I turned away from him. After Liam left, I shared his message with Bok-sun.

Bok-sun wasn't convinced. "We can't go. Remember how Auntie always said that the American soldiers are even more brutal than the Japanese? We're thousands of miles away from Korea right now. This island isn't even very close to the main Philippine island. We can't speak the local language, so where would we go even if we did run away? The Japanese were the ones who brought us here, so they'll have to send us home even if they lose the war."

I thought that Bok-sun might be right. Auntie and Uncle had always told us that the Americans would torture and kill us if they caught us.

The next day, Liam once again begged me to believe him and assured me that the American weren't bad people. But I agreed with Bok-sun that the Japanese would have to send us home.

About three days after Liam urged us to flee, the roar of airplanes filled the sky. Ten or so airplanes were flying toward the comfort station. Lights flashed under their wings, and fire blazed up around the field hospital. Auntie and Uncle scurried around to pack their things. The comfort women were in a panic, unsure of what to do.

"Hurry to the air raid shelter!" Uncle shouted.

The women rushed out of the hut and made a dash for

the shelter. Bok-sun and I held hands as we ran. Every bomb that fell sprayed dirt into the air. We all crowded under the tin roof of the shelter. Every time a bomb went off, my heart skipped a beat.

Bok-sun and I were clutching each other there in the air raid shelter when we heard Liam shouting at the top of his lungs. "Get out of the shelter right now! It's even more dangerous inside than outside. The tin roof is visible from up there in the bombers! Hurry up! They're dropping more bombs!"

I grabbed Bok-sun's hand and pulled her out of the shelter. Liam was frantically waving toward us, and we sprinted toward him. Then there was an earth-shattering roar that hurled me to the ground in a daze. Lumps of dirt rained down on me. I thought I was dead until somebody grabbed my arm. It was Liam. He was covered in so much dirt I could hardly tell if he was a man or a monster.

"We've got to get going! Over here!"

Liam pulled me away from the air raid shelter. Another bomb fell, uprooting trees and filling the air with dirt and dust. Bok-sun was nowhere to be seen.

"Bok-sun! We've got to find her. Bok-sun, where are you?"

I wildly ran back toward the shelter to look for her. While I was on my way, the tin roof vanished in a sheet of fire. The blast knocked me over, sending chunks of earth and acrid smoke in all directions. I'd barely regained my senses and gotten back on my feet when I saw what looked like a big black clump of dirt rolling toward me. It was Bok-sun. I flung my arms around her. My momentary joy at finding her alive was interrupted by Auntie and Uncle, who called to us as they clawed their way from beneath a hill of dirt.

"This way! We've got to get to the field hospital!"

Only five of the comfort women had survived—Umiko, Junko, and Miyako, along with Bok-sun and I. Learning that the rest of the women had died in the air raid shelter gave me the chills. Auntie yelled at us to pick up our things. We dashed back into the hut and grabbed our bundles of clothing. There was no telling when the bombers would return. Liam helped us make our way toward the field hospital.

When we reached the hospital, foul-smelling smoke blanketed the area. There were gaping holes in the walls of the building, through which we could see the wounded soldiers moaning inside. The hospital director and most of the officers had already fled. The wounded soldiers and the doctor were rushing to pack their things.

When Uncle asked for a truck, the doctor said, "They took all the trucks when they fled. They didn't leave a single one behind."

A Japanese soldier—an officer, I guessed, given the stars on his shoulder—spoke up. "The bombing is so intense it might be even more dangerous to be in a truck. We've got to move into the jungle."

"What do we do with the injured soldiers?"

"Only take the ones that can move!"

Hearing this, the wounded soldiers raised a clamor and stretched out their hands toward us imploringly. Some of them had amputated legs, and others couldn't see because of bandages wrapped around their heads. Liam, who had followed us into the hospital, ran over to the wounded soldiers to comfort them.

But just then, the officer raised his gun and began firing at the wounded soldiers. When Liam gestured at the officer to stop shooting, a bullet struck him in the chest. Liam fell to the ground, his arms jerking. I hurried over to him. Blood oozed from his mouth.

"Liam! Liam!"

Liam grabbed my hand, and his lips moved. He seemed to be trying to tell me something.

I leaned over and whispered into his ear. "No, Liam! Don't leave us."

"The coast… go to the coast. At the coast, the Americans … the Americans will take… will take you…" Before Liam could finish the sentence, his head sagged backward.

I shook him and shouted, "Liam, no! Oh, no!"

Then the officer who'd shot Liam leveled his gun at me. "Hurry up!" he shouted.

Bok-sun dashed over and tugged on my arm. I didn't want to leave Liam there. It was all so horrible that I couldn't even work up any tears. Against my will, Bok-sun dragged me along after the departing soldiers. I couldn't get Liam's face out of my mind.

I'm sorry, Liam. I'm so sorry. Those vicious brutes! How could they just gun someone down who'd served them so well?

It hurt me to leave Liam's body lying there on the ground like that, since he'd always been so kind to me. But there was no way of knowing when the Japanese soldiers would turn their guns on us, too. Auntie and Uncle shouted to us to catch up with the group.

We were on a rough jungle path that was barely wide enough to walk down in single file. The jungle was teeming with venomous spiders and leeches.

We walked on and on, until the ache in my feet became unbearable. Any farther, I thought, and I might fall down and not be able to get back up. With Bok-sun's help, I managed to stay on my feet. The other three women were gasping as well. The humidity made it hard to breathe. I was dripping with sweat, and my legs trembled. I kept thinking that Liam would show up any minute with a big grin on his face.

Even though we'd walked all day long, the jungle dragged on. With the sky blocked by the canopy of trees, it was hard to tell if it was day or night. We had to keep walking even when we ate. I guessed we were short on supplies, because Auntie barely fed us enough to take the edge off our appetite.

On the third day, the sky slowly came into view, and the mountains, too. We seemed to be finally getting clear of the jungle. The Japanese soldiers told us we had to cross the mountains before we could reach the ocean. I remembered how Liam had murmured with his dying breath that we should go to the coast and find an American ship. To encourage us, Auntie told us we'd be able to board a Japanese ship that was evacuating the troops. The thought of a ship waiting to take us home gave us the energy to push forward a little harder.

Now that we were on the outskirts of the jungle, the blazing sun beat down on us. When the sun was high overhead, Bok-sun, who was walking in front of me, suddenly keeled over. In shock, I tried to help her up, but her body just sagged back against my arms. There was something off about her eyes, too.

"Bok-sun, what's the matter? Wake up!"

"Auntie, something's wrong with Bok-sun!" I shouted.

Auntie, who was up ahead of us, looked back with a frown on her face. "Huh? What is it?"

"Bok-sun fainted."

Auntie and Uncle exchanged looks and then spoke together in a low voice.

"There's nothing we can do for her. We've got to hurry," Uncle said and nudged Auntie onward without even looking back.

"We can't do that! Hang on a minute!"

The other three comfort women helped me pick up Bok-sun and put her on my back. In the meantime, the marching Japanese soldiers were getting farther away. Uncle ran up to the soldiers and told them something.

Just when we started to move forward, carrying Bok-sun, the Japanese soldiers turned around, cursing at us and raising their guns. All of a sudden, the image of Liam bleeding on the ground flashed through my mind.

"Everyone, run for it! Into the jungle!"

With Bok-sun still on my back, the four of us ran back into the jungle as quick as lightning. I was shocked by my own strength. Behind us, we heard the rattle of gunfire—the soldiers were firing at us. By the time we ran out of breath, we'd reached a thick section of the jungle, far off the trail. We crouched down and lay flat against the earth.

There were a few more gunshots, and then the jungle grew quiet.

As I laid Bok-sun down on the ground, I spotted a huge centipede skittering past me. It was only then that I remembered where we were—deep in the jungle, which was infested with venomous insects. In terror, we crawled out of the jungle, pulling Bok-sun along with us. When we had a moment to collect ourselves, I noticed that our feet were torn and bleeding from the brambles we'd run through. Until that moment, I hadn't felt any pain.

Bok-sun squinted and looked around.

"She's waking up!" The four of us clustered around her.

"Where are we? What happened to the soldiers?" Bok-sun asked.

I envied the fact that she didn't seem to remember a thing. "Bok-sun, didn't you hear the gunshots? Those damn Japanese tried to kill us!"

Miyako spoke up. "I heard the soldiers grumbling about how we were short on food. That was around the time they gunned down the wounded men. Running away was the right decision. It's a good thing we're here in the jungle. Otherwise, the soldiers would have tracked us down and killed us."

Bok-sun sighed. "It sounds like I nearly got you all killed! Well, what do we do now?"

I was so glad that Bok-sun was back to her old self. "We have to find the ocean now. That's where Liam told us to go—to the American army."

Escaping from the Japanese soldiers had taken a load off our shoulders. We started moving slowly toward the coast, but stayed on the lookout for the Japanese. I thought about the story I'd heard from the young soldier who'd visited my room. During a retreat, he'd told me, the Japanese had slaughtered all the Korean workers and comfort women. We were extremely fortunate to have gotten away from the Japanese, despite our close brush with death.

Though Bok-sun was awake again, she was still too dizzy to walk without our help. As we looked for a place to rest, I took a closer look at Bok-sun. It seemed clear she was suffering from sunstroke, caused by the sudden exposure to intense sunlight in her weak condition. She'd lost a lot of blood during the stabbing and then hadn't gotten enough to eat during her recovery.

Umiko took the lead. "First things first: we've got to find something to eat. Bok-sun, you need to rest here in the shade while you get your energy back. You'll be right as rain in no time," she said.

Umiko took Junko and Miyako with her to find some food and left me to look after Bok-sun.

"Don't go too far," I told the three women. I found some

fresh water for Bok-sun and wet her lips with it.

"Those awful Japanese soldiers are gone now. Once we get to the coast and find the Americans, we'll be able to go home. Cheer up, Bok-sun!"

While looking after Bok-sun, I listened carefully to the sounds of the jungle.

I wonder if we'll be able to find the American army on the coast. I hope we don't run into those Japanese soldiers again while we're wandering through the mountains!

I was so nervous that the slightest wind could have made me tremble. I found myself wishing I'd run off with Bok-sun when Liam urged me to. If I'd known what would happen, I would've listened to him, and then he wouldn't have died.

If only Liam were still alive!

I was still tormented by the fact that we hadn't gotten to bury his body.

In a little while, the three women who'd gone looking for provisions returned with bananas and breadfruit. It was such a relief to see them. After scarfing down some food, we finally felt a little better.

We agreed to stay there for a few more days, until Bok-sun had regained her strength, and to take turns looking for food. Over the next five days, Bok-sun gradually regained her strength.

"From now on, let's call ourselves by our real names," I suggested. "I'm not Haruko; I'm Heo Chun-ja."

This prompted Bok-sun to reveal her real name, too. "OK. I'm not Fumiko. I'm Kim Bok-sun."

"My name isn't Umiko, it's Mi-sun, Choe Mi-sun."

"And I'm not Junko; I'm Kkeut-nyeo. My family name is Park."

"My real name's Sam-rye, not Miyako. Oh Sam-rye."

Calling each other by our real names seemed to give us new energy.

We set out once again in search of the coast. Reaching the crest of a low hill, we saw another mountain ahead of us. Though we weren't sure which direction we should go, we kept walking and walking, with the hope that crossing these mountains would eventually bring us to the sea. When we spotted a tender-looking vine on the side of the road, we'd tear it off and dribble some of the sap in front of a line of ants. If the ants stopped to drink the sap, we figured it was safe for us to chew on the vine.

About halfway up the mountain, we came upon a long sword sticking out of a big tree. It was the type of sword used by the Japanese.

Japanese soldiers must have passed by here. Some of them might still be lurking around!

We found a hiding spot and waited to see if someone

would come back for the sword. But nearly a whole day passed without any sign of human presence. We finally relaxed when we got a closer look at the sword: moss was growing on the handle, and the blade was rusty. The sword was a real prize, since it helped us cut through branches and clear away brambles in our way.

We'd barely managed to reach the top of another hill when we seemed to hear people talking. Nervously, we held our breath and strained to listen.

Waiting for a Ship

On the coast, 1945

There was no doubt: we were hearing human voices.

I wonder who they could be!

We were frightened not only of Japanese soldiers but also of the natives of this country. In fact, we were frightened by the very idea of people. Taking cover, we waited to see who was talking. We could indistinctly see two men off to the side, behind a big boulder. The clothing they were wearing had the color and design of Japanese uniforms. One of the men was lying down, as if sick, while the other walked with a limp. From our hiding place, we breathlessly waited to see what they would do.

Are these the soldiers that left behind that sword? Did they get separated in the retreat, like us? Are there only two of them?

Since neither of the men seemed to be in good health,

I thought we could outrun them, as long as they weren't armed. But where there are soldiers, there are always guns. Anxiously, we kept watching them. I figured that the man on the ground must be wounded, because I hadn't seen him get up even once.

The man with the limp squatted down for a moment and then picked up a gun and turned in our direction, nearly scaring us to death.

Did he see us?

Then the man on the ground said something. We pricked up our ears.

"What was that?" the other man said.

"I said, don't go off too far!"

The two were speaking Korean! We scrambled to our feet with joy. Catching sight of us, the man with the limp pointed his gun at us.

"Don't move!"

The words were like music to my ears. In near unison, the other women and I shouted, "Just a second! We're Koreans!"

"Huh? What's going on here? We thought you were a bunch of ghosts!"

Once we got closer to the two men, I saw that the man with the limp was around my age. It was a big relief to run into Koreans out here.

Just as the men had said, we were a sorry sight indeed. Our clothes were tattered and torn from our trek through the jungle, and our uncombed hair was a total mess. No wonder the men had thought we were ghosts.

"The two of you don't look much better!" I shot back.

This got a chuckle from the man on the ground. Through his shaggy beard, I caught a glimpse of rotten yellow teeth. His military uniform was even more ragged than the ones we were wearing. The two men looked malnourished. It couldn't have been easy for them to find food in the jungle, considering they were both injured.

"How long have you two been out here?"

The man with the limp responded. "I guess it's been more than a month now. We were on the run from the bombers, just like you. During the escape, my friend here fell into a ravine and hurt his back. That night, we heard the officer telling the soldiers they should get rid of us. He said they couldn't take an injured soldier with them and didn't have enough supplies for us anyway. After hearing that, I waited until the middle of the night and then stole out of the camp with my friend on my back. Otherwise, I have no doubt that those soldiers would've killed us. They herded a group of comfort women into a cave and then blew them all up with grenades."

"No way? With grenades?"

"That's right. Damn those Japanese! I guess they went to the trouble of killing those women because they were afraid their crimes would come to light if they survived. Whatever happens, don't let yourselves get caught by the Japanese again. We've seen for ourselves what they're capable of."

That story gave me goosebumps. If Bok-sun hadn't fainted from sunstroke, the Japanese soldiers might have killed us all on the excuse that there wasn't enough food.

"The Japanese soldiers at the field hospital said we should go to the coast and find a Japanese warship to take us home. What are you planning to do? We're trying to meet up with the Americans."

"We were looking for the Americans, too," said the man with the limp. "But I hurt my leg while I was carrying my friend, which is why we're holed up here. We're a lot better than we were before."

"How far are we from the coast?"

"We're not sure either. But considering that the planes come from over that way to drop their bombs and then fly back that way when they're done, we can only assume there's an Allied base over there."

That evening, we shared our bananas and breadfruit with the two men and debated our course of action late into the night.

The man with the injured back said, "It would be dangerous for us all to stick together. Some of the Japanese may still be out there. If we're all in a big group, we're more likely to be discovered. So you women should head out right away. I think the ocean is on the other side of that ridge. If you want to find the American army, you've got to head to the coast."

"So what are you two going to do? You can't even walk!"

"We've decided to take our chances here. If you find the Americans down by the coast, please let them know there are some Koreans up in the mountains who could use a little help!"

"Do you think the American soldiers will hurt us?"

The man with the injured back shook his head. "When you find the Americans, be sure to tell them you're 'Korean.' If they say anything about 'Japan,' you have to say you're 'Korean,' not 'Japanese.' As long as you do that, you should be fine. Remember to say 'Korean'!"

He had us repeat the English words several times until we were sure we could remember them.

After bringing the two men an ample supply of breadfruit and bananas, we set out once more on our journey. No matter how far we walked, the mountains seemed endless. We would rest in the shade at noon, when the sun was blazing, and then start moving again once it cooled off. After walking for what felt like ages, I'd turn around only to see our last resting place right behind us. It was a constant cycle of walking and resting. During our breaks, we'd sit down until we got a second wind and then hit the trail once more.

When the straps on our clogs wore out on the arduous mountain trails, we'd tear off tough strips of tree bark and twist them into strings for our shoes. But we wouldn't get very far before those strings would snap, too. Our clothes had become so ragged by this point that our skin peeked out through the holes. On our meager diet, we lost so much weight that we looked like sticks draped in rags as we tottered along.

We wanted to hurry, but our feet were leaden. We guzzled water to fill our bellies and nibbled on edible shoots we found along the way. Eating the wrong plant would cause a terrible stomachache and explosive diarrhea, and then we'd have to spend a few days resting until our bodies recovered. Over time, experience taught us which leaves and shoots were safe to eat, and which were not.

Despite walking for days, we didn't come across any signs of other people. We even started to wish we'd stayed with the Korean men we'd run into. As we wandered through the mountains, there was no way to know how many days had passed. Our main goals were finding something to eat when the sun came up and finding a safe place to sleep when it went down. Our long fingernails were our tools, and our long hair kept us warm at night. Our heads were infested with lice, which we could see wriggling around when we took a break. Our clothes were matted with sweat and dust and dirt, and they crackled like old leather. Several times, we almost headed back to where the men were staying, but each time we decided against it. We were sure the ocean was waiting for us just beyond the next ridge, but every time we only found more mountains.

One day, though, the wind felt different than usual. There was a tang of salt in the air. I'd spent more than a decade breathing in the sea breeze by Ganwoldo Island, which is probably why I recognized it at once.

"That's the sea breeze, no doubt about it! The ocean isn't far, now."

With each step, our pace got a little faster. Soon we reached the top of a low rise.

Ah, it was the ocean, at last! Before our eyes, the blue waters of the boundless ocean stretched out to the horizon, where it met the sky. There was nothing to see out there— no warships, no boats, no soldiers—nothing but the blue vastness. That was fine with me, though. I was happy simply to have reached the ocean.

As we raced down the slope toward the seashore, a thought suddenly struck me.

"We ought to be more alert now than ever! If there are

Japanese soldiers hiding out by the beach, we're in big trouble. The first thing we should do is find cover and see whether the area is clear."

So we all concealed ourselves behind palm trees. For quite a while, we kept watch on the beach. The sunlight danced on the white grains of sand, tiny fragments of seashells built up over the eons. I couldn't shake the feeling that armed soldiers would show up at any minute. But the only sound was the crash of the waves, and we couldn't see any signs of people.

"It's so quiet. It should be OK for us to relax now."

We headed straight for the water and jumped in, letting the seawater cover us from head to toe. Next to the beach was a grove of tall palm trees, and across from that a thicket of bamboo. We decided to set up camp in the shade beneath the palm trees.

After resting for a while, we got thirsty. We found water close by, in a stream flowing down from the hills into the sea. The next thing we needed was something to eat. I had the feeling we would find something in the bamboo thicket. As we got closer, we stumbled upon a pile of human skeletons. Crabs were scampering around the bones, as if playing hide and seek. We were less interested in the bones than the crabs, which we could eat. We pounced on the unsuspecting crabs and put them into a crude basket that we'd made by folding big leaves together. Soon enough, our leaf basket was stuffed with crabs.

After starting a fire with flint and steel, we wrapped the crabs in leaves and cooked them over the flames. Before long, the air was filled with the savory aroma of cooking crab. Though we were worried that the smoke might give us away to any soldiers lurking nearby, we couldn't resist our craving for cooked food—we'd gone without it for so long.

We began our feast without even waiting for the crabs to cool. My mouth was scorched by the hot meat and scraped by the hard shells, and soon both my gums and throat ached. After we finished the crabs, we were overtaken by an overwhelming fatigue. We spread out palm leaves on the ground beneath the palm trees and lay down there in the shade. Since we were in the tropics, there was no need for blankets. As soon as we lay down, we fell fast asleep.

How long was I out?

I'd been awakened by the drumbeat of the rain. Black storm clouds hemmed us in on all sides. In the jungle, there were torrential showers several times a day, but they never lasted very long.

By the time the rain stopped, I was starting to get a bellyache. It must've been because of the crab we'd gorged on. We all had diarrhea for several days, which left us without an ounce of energy. We could barely manage to crawl and scrounge around for breadfruit. Fortunately, we found bananas and mangos, too. To avoid getting sick again, we only ate a little crab and relied on bananas and breadfruit for our meals.

When we woke up in the morning, our most pressing question was finding enough to eat to make it through another day. We ate a wide range of things—anything edible that we could find. On some days it was sugar cane, and on other days, mangos. We gathered young shoots and caught more crabs. Despite being dressed in rags and often going hungry, we enjoyed complete freedom for the first time.

One day, after exhausting the resources near the beach, we decided to venture a little farther inland.

"Let's try climbing that hill today. We might see a ship from up there."

"All right. We should get a better view from up there."

We all climbed the hill. It wasn't that high, but when we reached the top, we could see far out to sea. There were no ships in sight.

"How come there aren't any ships out there?"

"Ships tend to stick to regular routes. Obviously, we're not on one of those routes."

"That's right. Even the sea has its roads, they say."

"What should we do, then? Should we keep moving until

we find one of those routes?

"Let's just wait here. There's fruit to eat, so we won't starve to death. A ship is bound to pass by at some point."

We'd grown accustomed to the beach with its palm trees and were afraid of going somewhere else.

There were more edible plants up on the hill than down by the beach. The plants reminded me of my early teens, when I used to nibble on the wild greens growing on the hill by our village.

My Friend Bok-sun

American naval vessel, 1945

By now, seven years had passed since I'd left home. I was the only one of the group who'd been gone for that long. Bok-sun had been carried off five years ago, and the others just a couple of years ago. I thought my mom must have cried her eyes out waiting for me.

If I boarded a ship sailing east from here, I wonder if it would eventually take me home.

Sitting there on top of the hill, I could've sworn I was on the hill behind my village. Staring out at the endless ocean, the other women and I briefly forgot about the war and chattered together like schoolgirls.

Mi-sun, who was the oldest of us, took a look around. "I wish we were in the hills by my village! The biggest mountain near my home is Mt. Gayasan. Every spring, we'd go up there to pick wild greens. There were bracken fiddleheads in the hills and castor aralia shoots in the valleys. The shady areas were just full of alpine knotweed. If knotweed grew here, we could pick that every day."

The very mention of knotweed made my mouth water.

Mi-sun said she was from Yesan, in Chungcheong Province. Her face blushing, she spoke timidly. "I was carried off right after they gave the national mobilization order. My parents rushed to marry off my two older sisters and were trying to find a match for me, too, when I was taken. That was just two years ago, but it feels like ages. You don't think I'm too old to find a man, do you? Ah, I wonder who my husband will be."

Bok-sun's lashes fluttered over her big eyes as she gazed off into the distance. "Five years ago, they took me to Shanghai and from there to Nanjing. I'd been promised to marry this young man named Jun-bae in the next village over from ours. My mom said our wedding would be held that fall, but I was kidnapped in the spring. I think Jun-bae is waiting for me even now. He called me the prettiest girl in the world."

Sam-rye fiddled with a lovely flower as she told us how she'd been taken from Jeongeup, in Jeolla Province. "If I hadn't been brought here, I would've gotten married to Ho-sik, one of our neighbors' servants. He told me he couldn't go a single day without seeing me, but I left without even saying goodbye. I'm sure he's waiting for me. When I get home, I'm going to marry him and live happily ever after."

As we relived the innocence of our youth, we couldn't stop talking about the men we dreamed of marrying.

"When I get married, I only want to have boys. I don't care for girls!" Sam-rye said.

Bok-sun shook her head. "I can't stand men. I'm only going to have pretty girls. If I have a daughter who looks like me, I bet Jun-bae will pamper her even more than me. I'll be happy if I only have daughters."

Kkeut-nyeo chimed in, with a blush on her comely cheeks. "The man I liked was from the town up the hill. His name is Deok-chil—which sounds a little lame, now that I think about it. We even held hands one time. Whenever I went into the woods to gather wild greens, he had a knack for suddenly showing up with an A-frame carrier on his back."

Sam-rye burst out laughing. "I'd say that Kkeut-nyeo is an even lamer name than Deok-chil!"

Kkeut-nyeo stuck her tongue out at Sam-rye crossly. "There's nothing that fancy about the name Sam-rye, either! My mom told me she named me Kkeut-nyeo, 'last girl,' because she'd only had daughters and was ready for some sons. I'd like to have a lot of kids, and I don't care whether they're boys or girls."

As I listened to the other women talk about their crushes from back home, I found myself thinking of Jin-gyu.

When I get home, will there be anyone waiting for me aside from Mom and Chun-sik? I wonder if Jin-gyu is back from Japan.

I wasn't sure if Jin-gyu shared my feelings about him. He was the only person from my village who'd gone to study in Japan.

What if Jin-gyu was drafted into the Japanese army like so many other students?

While I was lost in thought, Bok-sun asked me a question. "You were the first of us five to become a comfort woman, right? Didn't you say you were carried away at the age of thirteen?"

Mi-sun clucked her tongue.

Bok-sun's hands were shaking. "How stupid we were to fall for Japan's blatant lies!"

"We're not to blame," Sam-rye said. "There's nothing wrong with being innocent. It was those wicked liars who were in the wrong."

Mi-sun nodded in agreement and then turned to me. "What about you, Chun-ja? Was there a boy that you fancied?"

Without meaning to, Mi-sun's innocent question had touched a sore spot. Even if I did fancy someone, I couldn't get married—not without a uterus. Reminded of my terrible fate, I suddenly began to cry.

Bok-sun stroked my back to console me. "From now on, we have to keep quiet about everything we went through. Who could we tell about the horrible things we suffered? Only the sky above us and the earth below us will know the truth. If we'd known the terrible things they'd make us do, we would've died before following them. We were all tricked. That's why it's not our fault. What I'm saying is that we're just innocent victims. In the future, we deserve to be happy. That's how we get justice. No women on earth have suffered as we have. So we're owed twice the happiness of other women."

"That's right! We've got to find happiness."

For me, the word "happy" seemed extremely abstract.

What does it mean for a woman to be happy? Does happiness mean getting married and having children?

In that case, I could never be happy, since I'd never be able to have children. Perhaps the other women could move on with their lives if they kept their mouths shut about their past, but hiding my past wouldn't heal the awful wound I'd suffered.

Gnawing my lips, I stared out at the sea. My vision was blurred by the tears in my eyes.

For a while, everybody was silent. We still hadn't seen

any ships passing by.

Bok-sun got to her feet and addressed us all. "We'll be spending the rest of our lives making up for the awful things we've been through. It's time we got going. We haven't seen any ships today—not even the tip of a mast, for that matter. Let's pick some wild greens. We have to stay fed until a ship shows up."

This was the first time since leaving home that I'd been able to release the emotions I'd been suppressing, my longing for home and my hatred for the Japanese army.

I was brought back to earth by someone shouting in Japanese. "Don't move!"

In utter surprise, we spun around toward the voice. Two men were standing there, in ragged uniforms issued by the Japanese army, pointing guns at us. We froze in place, unable to move.

Where did they come from?

I guessed we'd been so lost in our reverie that we'd let our guard down. We were trapped, with no way out.

How could we let ourselves fall into their clutches again?

Ahead of us, there was a sheer cliff, with dark waves crashing far below. Behind us, there were the soldiers. There was nowhere to run.

The soldiers came closer, one step at a time. We edged back, toward the cliff.

"Where did you run off from?" one of the soldiers asked.

"We were abandoned by the Japanese army."

"Is there anyone else with you?"

We shook our heads.

"You're lucky they spared your lives. Hand over all the food you have!" the taller of the two soldiers said. His voice was weak, as if he'd gone several days without food. Obviously, the soldiers were stragglers who'd lost their way, just as we had. I wasn't about to let the Japanese have their way with me again, but it would also be rash to provoke them. The word "accommodating" flashed through my mind.

That's it! We should pretend to be accommodating.

I was filled with an unexpected boldness, probably because we had the numerical advantage.

"We have some breadfruit down there," I said, pointing toward the beach.

Bok-sun stared at me with wide eyes. I gave her a reassuring glance.

"Is there anyone there?"

"Nope, no one at all. That's where we've been staying."

"OK. Lead the way, and be quick about it."

The soldiers kept their guns pointed at us, with one soldier behind us and the other in front, as we walked down toward the beach.

"What are we going to do?" Mi-sun whispered. She was

shaking, and Sam-rye and Kkeut-nyeo's faces were as white as a sheet.

"As the old saying goes, if you keep your wits about you, you can even escape from a tiger's lair. Stay calm and don't piss them off," I said in a low voice, and Bok-sun nodded.

I wasn't sure where my courage had come from. Since there was no way to give the soldiers the slip or run away just then, we had to keep our eyes peeled for the right opportunity. We weren't about to just hand over the freedom we'd risked our lives to obtain. It was clear these soldiers were more worn out than we were.

I felt someone poke me in the ribs. It was Bok-sun, who was walking behind me.

"OK, Bok-sun. First, we'll give them something to eat, and once they're no longer on their guard..." I finished the sentence with a significant look. We walked at a deliberately slow pace, hoping the soldiers would think we were tired.

We came to the place where we'd been staying. But to our surprise, the palm leaves we'd covered the breadfruit with were all in disarray. And that wasn't all. The palm leaves we'd laid down for our bedding had been disturbed, too.

Did the soldiers already come through here?

I was struck with fear. The breadfruit was all gone. If the soldiers thought we'd lied to them, they could easily shoot us on the spot. Hesitantly, we checked under the palm leaves. Clearly, someone had taken not only the breadfruit but also our belongings. We looked around the area, trying to spot the breadfruit. Bok-sun was starting to get worried, but I told her to stay calm.

At that moment, one of the soldiers pointed the barrel of his gun at Bok-sun. "Hurry up with that food, and don't try to pull anything. After we eat, I think we're going to have a little fun—it's been long enough! You girls line up over there."

This made my hair stand on end. Bok-sun rummaged through the palm leaves, pretending to look for the breadfruit.

"We put the food here, but now it's gone!"

"What's wrong with you! Hand over your food, you *josenpi*!"

The Japanese soldier smashed the butt of his rifle down on Bok-sun's head and sent her sprawling. Then there was the crack of a rifle, and the soldier who'd hit Bok-sun fell to the ground.

"Dammit! They tricked us!" the other soldier said, aiming his rifle at Bok-sun.

"Everyone duck!" someone shouted in Korean.

There was another gunshot. The second Japanese soldier was hit in the leg and fell to the ground. His gun went off, and Bok-sun let out a scream. The next moment, there was a fourth gunshot, and blood spurted from the fallen soldier's chest.

The Korean men that we'd met in the mountains came out from behind the palm trees, carrying rifles. I ran over to Bok-sun, where she lay bleeding, and took her in my arms.

Bok-sun's lips moved, as if she were trying to say something. But instead of words, blood dripped from her mouth.

"No, Bok-sun! You have to wake up!"

A few moments later, Bok-sun's head slumped backward.

"You can't die like this! Come on, open your eyes!"

Bok-sun would never open her eyes again. As I held her close, my body shook violently.

"Bok-sun is dead, and it's all because of those two men!"

"I feel so bad for her," one of the men said. "I wish we'd finished off those bastards sooner."

Mi-sun comforted me. "There was nothing they could do. If it weren't for them, we might all have been killed. Don't cry, Chun-ja."

"What do we do now? Bok-sun! Bok-sun!" I felt so sad to lose my friend.

The Korean men told us that when they'd stumbled upon our camp, they'd assumed that Japanese soldiers were staying there. So they'd made a meal of the breadfruit we'd stored there and then gone into hiding. If it weren't for the two of them, we might've suffered terrible things. The men helped us bury Bok-sun on a sand dune. We buried the Japanese soldiers' bodies, too. They'd been our enemies, but given our common humanity, they deserved our pity, too.

"It's just so unfair. Why did Bok-sun have to die like that? Surely it was enough to be taken thousands of miles from home and treated terribly by the Japanese soldiers. She didn't deserve to die on top of that!"

As we buried Bok-sun, the other women and I wept until our eyes became red and swollen. At first, I cried with sadness and rage at Bok-sun's death, but eventually I cried because of our awful fate.

After that, we took turns standing watch on the beach. If anyone saw a passing ship, they were supposed to throw their hands into the air. The people who weren't standing watch went around looking for food.

Ten or so days later, I was on duty, gazing intently at the glittering ocean and determined not to get distracted. I was afraid that, if I let my eyes wander for even one moment, a ship would pass by and disappear before I could spot it.

All of a sudden, I saw a dot moving on the horizon. I rubbed my eyes and looked again. My heart pounded in my chest. The dot began to get bigger. It looked like a pointed flag, or the wings of a huge bird. It kept growing until it looked like a ship. Then I was sure—it *was* a ship.

Somehow, I had to send a signal to that ship. I had to let

the crew know that we needed to be rescued. I beckoned to the ship with all my strength. There wasn't a minute—not a second—to lose. I wasn't sure whether the crew had spotted me, but the ship didn't change course. I slipped out of my ragged clothes and whirled them around above my head. Even so, the ship held to its course. I ran around on the beach, waving my clothes and yelling at the top of my lungs.

"Help! Over here!"

The others were out looking for food, but my shouting brought them sprinting back to the beach. They ripped off their tattered clothes and waved them at the ship, too. We were so desperate that our shouting soon turned to wailing. For a while, the ship seemed to be getting closer, then it moved farther away.

Maybe they didn't see us.

The two men ran into the water and shouted their heads off. We threw our energy into waving our arms.

"What about shooting the guns?" I shouted to the men. "If they hear gunshots, don't you think they'll come this way?"

"Shooting the guns is too risky, because they might think we're the enemy. If they fire their naval guns at us, we'll be blown to smithereens."

We kept frantically waving our clothes. The ship changed

direction and began moving toward us. It looked like our rescue was at hand. The ship slowly drew closer. We waved more vigorously and shouted for help.

At last, we could see people on the deck of the ship. We threw our arms around each other and cried tears of joy.

Then there was the crack of gunfire, and we dashed in terror toward the bamboo thicket.

Why would they shoot at us when we're asking for help?

When the ship we'd been waiting for so eagerly started shooting at us, our excitement turned into despair. Hiding among the bamboo stalks, we watched the ship. The gunfire soon stopped.

Are they Japanese or Americans? What if the Americans do bad things to us?

In a little while, we saw a boat being lowered from the ship.

I wonder if that boat is coming to get us. What now? Should we hide in the jungle again?

If the boat turned out to be filled with Japanese and we fell into their hands, they would make us do those awful things again, and I couldn't bear the thought of that.

"We should wait until they get closer. If they're Americans, we'll run right toward them. If they're Japanese, we'll flee into the jungle."

Breathlessly, we crouched down in the bamboo thicket,

trying to stay calm. The sailors on the boat came into view. They looked taller than the Japanese, and their uniforms were a different color. Without a doubt, they were Americans.

"They must be Americans! Let's all wave at them!"

The women and I ran onto the beach, as the men limped along behind us. The American sailors gestured to us from the boat, urging us to move toward the boat.

"Everyone, raise your hands in the air and shout, 'Korean!'"

We moved toward the boat, shouting the word over and over. The sailors held out their hands and motioned us to get in. As we boarded the boat, we shed tears of joy. The sailors spoke to us in a mixture of English and Korean.

"You're Korean? Is there anyone else?"

We just nodded happily.

"Is it just the six of you? No Japanese?"

"No, we all ran away. It's just us."

The sailors nodded, and the boat took us toward the ship.

A rope ladder was let down from the ship. One at a time, the sailors helped us climb up the ladder. Sure enough, it was an American naval vessel. Once we were all aboard, the sailors took us to a cabin.

When the people in the cabin saw us, they gasped in

shock and murmured to themselves. They asked us some questions, but we just shook our heads, unable to understand them.

The sailors gave each of us a military outfit and a small box. The sailor who spoke some Korean came in and told us to eat the food in the box and get changed.

The box contained field rations: a biscuit, beef jerky, sugar, cheese, and dried fruit. I'd never had food like that before. While I ate the rations, I wept at the thought of Boksun, buried on the beach.

If those Japanese soldiers hadn't shown up, you could've been rescued just like us!

Next, we changed our clothes. The uniforms were way too big for us, as baggy as a burlap sack. But at least they kept us decent, unlike the rags we'd been wearing for so long.

After a few hours, the ship stopped. The sailors let the boat down again and had us board it. The Korean men joined us at this point, but we could barely recognize them, because they'd had a chance to shave their beards. Looking at each other's faces, we joked about how we finally looked human again.

The Americans took us to a tent on the beach, where we were questioned by soldiers who told us that we were POWs, prisoners of war. The men were questioned in a separate room. During the questioning, we learned about the latest developments. It turned out that we had crossed to the other side of Leyte Island. A few months ago, the Americans and Japanese had fought a fierce battle there, and the Japanese forces had been destroyed by heavy bombing. The Japanese soldiers we'd encountered on the beach were among the scattered remnants of the island's garrison.

We were all questioned under our Japanese names. The interrogators asked us where we'd come from, when and where we'd been taken, where we'd stayed, how long we'd been at the beach, and how many of us there had been at first. We told the Americans everything that had happened after the bombing had begun: fleeing with the Japanese soldiers from the field hospital, going off on our own, living by the beach, running into the Japanese soldiers, and Bok-sun getting killed. The Americans told us to put a thumbprint above our names, and we did as we were told.

After the questioning was over, the American soldiers loaded us into a jeep.

"Where are you taking us?" I found it hard to relax, still afraid that the Americans would treat us as badly as the Japanese had.

"We're taking you to the POW camp."

"What happens there?"

"That's where the Japanese prisoners of war are being

kept."

I was frightened to hear that Japanese would be there, too. "I won't go. I don't want to be with the Japanese soldiers. They'll do bad things to us again."

The interpreter shook his head. "You'll be OK there. The men are kept in a separate area. Those things aren't going to happen anymore."

Prisoners of War

POW camp in Manila, 1945

When we reached the POW camp, the buildings were divided into separate rooms. That put me on edge, since it reminded me of the comfort station. There were two bunk beds in each room, with the beds on opposite sides of the room. I glanced around the room to see if there was a bucket of water, a basin, or disinfectant. There was a square table by the window, but no sign of the things I was afraid of.

"For the time being, you'll be staying at this prisoner-of-war camp. You'll be safe here. In a little while, it will be dinner time. After you're done eating, you can relax," the interpreter said. He left the room and then locked the door from the outside.

Why do they lock the door here?

It looked like we didn't have the freedom to go outside when we wanted. In a little while, a woman came by with some outfits. She said they were the POW uniforms and told us to change into them. After getting changed, we lay down on the beds. I could hardly remember the last time I'd laid down on something so comfortable. Being able to relax made me feel like a new person.

Has that horrible lifestyle really come to an end?

As I was thinking about everything we'd experienced, I heard the door being unlocked. I sprang to my feet, terrified that a wicked soldier was about to enter. The painful memories I carried around inside me would sometimes pop into my head and make me panic.

The door opened, and a woman walked in. "Relax, everyone—I'm a Korean POW, too. Come and get something to eat."

I nearly cried with joy to see another Korean. "Is the war over?"

"It'll be over soon. You women are just skin and bones! How long did you go without food?"

"We got lost while we were retreating with the Japanese troops," I said, unwilling to tell the whole truth.

"Japan will have to surrender before long. When the war is over, we can go back home."

"Really? Will the American army send us home?"

"They will. But first of all, you need to get some food in your bellies. In your current condition, you'd probably keel over on your way home."

I was overcome with emotion.

The thought of the rice in the cafeteria made me think of Bok-sun once again.

"Let's go get some food," I told the other women. "We need to make sure we're strong enough to get home."

The other women felt the same way as I did.

The rice, side dishes, and soup in the cafeteria were a feast for us, the best meal we'd had since being taken by the Japanese. There was enough rice for everyone to have their fill, but I'd only managed to eat a little before my stomach ran out of room. Someone explained that I'd been hungry for so long that my stomach had shrunk in size.

The next day, we were taken to the hospital, where we were diagnosed with a whole battery of medical conditions. The hospital staff chopped off our hair, rubbed ointment on our sores, and even doused us in some kind of white powder. It was the first time since leaving home that I'd gotten any decent treatment.

Our questioning went on for several days. My interrogator focused on where I'd been and what I'd done. I couldn't bring myself to admit that I'd been a comfort woman, so I made up a story about working at the field hospital. The interrogator asked me a lot of detailed questions—how many people had been at the hospital, which way the Japanese troops had gone, how large their unit had been, and whether we'd been treated harshly—and wrote down my answers. I didn't say a thing about my time as a comfort woman. But keeping silent didn't heal the wounds in my heart.

There was a large yard outside our room in the camp. Every few days, the staff let us go outside to get some sunlight. There was a guard, but we could talk freely with the other POWs. The women were from various countries: China, Taiwan, the Philippines, Burma, Indonesia, and Singapore. There were also a lot of women from Japan. Most of the women socialized with people from their own country. The Japanese women didn't leave their rooms very much.

Looking at the other women, I wondered whether they'd all been comfort women like us. I didn't dare to ask them about it at first, but I got the feeling that they'd gone through the same things. Over time, there was more mingling among the women at the camp. I gradually got to know some of the women from other countries, and we soon found ourselves talking about our past. The fact that we'd suffered the same things made it easy for us to open to each other.

Most of the comfort women had frightful scars on their bodies. They'd been burned and stabbed in their breasts, backs, and thighs for fighting back or trying to run away. I was reminded of the scar on Bok-sun's chest. It always made me cry to think about how she'd been burned with a red-hot iron and how she'd been buried so far from home.

Thanks to the solid meals served at the camp, the women who'd been there a while had put on some weight and looked quite healthy. When they saw how emaciated we were, they asked us where we'd been and what had happened to us. They were all shocked to hear how we'd fled into the jungle and gotten lost there.

"You should've gone into town and found the American base. Why did you go into the jungle? It's so dangerous there!"

"We were staying at a field hospital in the middle of the jungle. The hospital was the only thing around there. We had no idea how to get into town."

"Well, at least you survived! Lots of people lost their way in the jungle and didn't make it out alive. If you hadn't been found by that American ship, you would've died there."

Once again, I regretted not listening to Liam when he'd urged me to run away and join the Americans. I was reminded of the skeletons scattered in the bamboo grove on the beach where we'd stayed. If we hadn't been rescued, our bones would've eventually been added to that pile.

After a while, we were relocated to a larger POW camp. We had much more liberty there than at the previous camp. The doors on our rooms weren't locked, and we could go out to the yard to play sports.

At the new camp, we had to go through another detailed interrogation. An American interpreter was with us while we were being questioned. The interpreter told us that we were Japanese POWs and therefore would be treated as war criminals, just like the Japanese. That shocked me. We were victims of the Japanese army, and we certainly hadn't been fighting for them! I realized it had been a huge mistake to hide my work as a comfort woman and make up a story about being a nurse at the field hospital during the first round of questioning. I decided to tell the whole truth during the second interrogation—that I was Korean and that my name wasn't Haruko, but Heo Chun-ja.

I told my roommates at the POW camp that they should tell the truth, too. As far as I could tell, that was the only way to convince the Americans that we should be treated differently from the Japanese POWs. There was a stark difference between us and the Japanese: the Japanese had started the war, and we'd been treated awfully by the Japanese. I encouraged the other women to declare that we'd been deceived by the Japanese and brought there by force, that we'd been forced to serve the soldiers' depraved whims against our will.

I told the women that we shouldn't be ashamed of ourselves. We should be enraged, not ashamed, that we'd fallen victim to a malicious lie and been brought here to suffer the most degrading treatment imaginable. The more ashamed we felt, the more pitiful and miserable our plight would be. We weren't war criminals who deserved punishment; we were the victims of Japans' war, and as such we deserved protection and compensation. Mi-sun came to see things my way and tried to win over Sam-rye and Kkeut-nyeo, too.

During the questioning, I told the American interrogator the truth about everything. I told him how, at the age of thirteen, I'd been promised a job at a textile mill and then forced onto a truck. I told him how I'd been taken to Inner Mongolia—instead of Japan, as I'd been led to believe—where I was raped by Japanese soldiers before I'd even started menstruating. I described in detail how the Pacific War had begun around the time of my first period, how we'd been driven to Shanghai and then taken by ship to Manila, and how I'd nearly died at sea.

During my physical exam, the interrogator asked me about the scars on my abdomen. As I told him about the most painful thing that had ever happened to me, my whole body trembled with rage at Japan.

"They cruelly ripped out my womb, so I can never become a mother. I tried to kill myself several times, but I just couldn't do it. The Japanese are fiends with human faces.

They should pay for tricking innocent girls like me into going to a war zone and for the horrible things they did to us there."

I couldn't go on. I could hardly breathe; my lungs ached; my fists clenched; my toes curled; my voice failed me. The startled interrogator gave me a sedative. I hadn't imagined it would be so painful to talk about the things I'd suffered.

The interrogator waited for me to take the sedative before speaking. "Good god! That's awful. I'm really sorry about bringing up your painful past. That's enough for today."

Even the American interpreter was teary-eyed.

While I was being questioned, I didn't want to talk to anyone else. I was afraid my resolution would waver. There were some pregnant POWs at the camp, and seeing them was a painful reminder that I couldn't have children. The way out of that pain was thinking about my dear mom and Chun-sik and remembering my childhood and my hometown.

Thinking about home brought to mind the salt tang of oysters. The wind blowing in from the ocean had carried the sulfurous odor of pine resin. But even the odors I remembered weren't as refreshing as they once had been, since they were tainted with pain.

A few weeks after my interrogation, I was awakened in

the middle of the night by what sounded like bombs going off all around us. In sheer terror, the other women and I threw open the door and ran outside. I'd thought the POW camp was being bombarded, but what I saw instead were dazzling streaks of color painting the night sky.

There was cheering all around us. We were told that the Japanese emperor had surrendered and that the war was over at last. What we were hearing wasn't bombs, but the crackle of fireworks being set off to celebrate the victorious end of the war. There was a festive mood on the streets of Manila, with Filipinos and American soldiers dancing and hugging everyone they met. Inside the camp, the POWs were split into two distinct groups: everyone was joyful except for the Japanese women, who huddled together, crying quietly with their heads bowed.

In a way, learning that the war was over was even more frustrating, since I wasn't sure how to get home. We had nothing to our name. We'd assumed we'd be departing on the journey home within a couple of days, but weeks passed without any changes.

About a month after we heard about the emperor surrendering, the American soldiers loaded all the POWs at the camp into trucks. We were taken to another POW camp on the coast.

We'd been there for about ten days when a huge ship,

with what seemed like three or four decks, steamed into the harbor. Seeing the ship filled us with excitement. My heart was already soaring through the skies of my childhood. We boarded a boat and were transferred to the ship. There were a large number of Japanese women, soldiers, and civilian contractors for the Japanese military aboard, so my friends and I found a spot near the other Koreans.

The scene aboard the ship was a complete reversal from our voyage in the opposite direction. The Koreans were chatting together boisterously, while the Japanese cowered in the corners and eyed us fearfully. Several people were so excited that they tearfully embraced each other.

At last, the ship began to move. Gazing out at the ocean, I tearfully relived the nightmare of the past years. As the coastline rapidly receded into the distance, my heart ached with the thought that Bok-sun hadn't survived.

On our return journey, the ship plowed through the waves with a swiftness that would've been unimaginable on our trip from Shanghai to Hong Kong and on to Manila. A few days later, the ship docked at a harbor on the island of Taiwan. After unloading Chinese POWs and picking up some Korean POWs on the island, we set off once more. Our destination, we were told, was the Japanese city of Shimonoseki. I'd assumed the ship would take us to Busan, and it made me very nervous to hear we were headed for Japan.

I had no idea how I'd be able to get home from Japan, since I couldn't afford to pay for the passage.

Mom, I'm Home

Home, 1946

Within a few days, our ship reached the harbor of Shimonoseki, and I finally set foot on Japanese soil. When I'd left home for what I'd thought would be a job at a textile mill in Japan, little did I dream that I'd be gone for eight years and suffer such terrible things.

My three friends and I held hands, both to comfort each other for the loss we felt and to ensure we didn't get separated.

"If you're headed to Korea, please gather over here," a voice said over a megaphone.

A guide took us to an inn, where a large number of women had already gathered. The women had been raped by the Japanese troops, just as we had. But I definitely wasn't ready to share the things I'd suffered with others. The only person I'd managed to tell everything to was the

American interrogator at the POW camp.

We were told we'd be boarding a ship bound for Busan early the next morning. Just hearing the word "Busan" felt as thrilling as actually getting home. Squeezed in with the other women, we stayed up almost the whole night.

The next day, our guide handed out rice balls and told us to come outside as soon as we'd eaten. When we reached the dock, it was already packed with people. The guide, who'd intended to put us on a ship, told us there weren't any more tickets and that we'd have to wait a little longer at the inn. The ships weren't able to accommodate all the Koreans trying to get home, which gave me some idea of just how many had been kidnapped by the Japanese. I wanted to get away from Japan as soon as possible, but I had to wait until tickets to Busan became available.

In a couple of days, we headed back down to the harbor, where once again the dock was crowded with people. Thanks to the POW agreement, we were able to board one of the American military vessels. But people who were trying to get back to Korea on their own were tearing out their hair trying to arrange passage.

The military vessel we were on set out for Busan. There were a lot of men on the ship who'd been drafted into the Japanese army and survived the perils of the battlefield. There were a lot of women on the ship, too, and they all had a sad look about them.

Tomorrow, I guess my dreams about going home will finally come true.

"We're on our way home at last!" Mi-sun said, her voice filled with relief. "But why do I feel so jumpy and have this tightness in my chest? How are all of you feeling?"

"I feel just like you! I ought to be delighted, but I feel a tightness in my chest."

"I can't seem to stop trembling. What's the matter with me?" said Kkeut-nyeo, the youngest of us, as she wiped tears from her eyes. I felt the same way.

How am I going to look Mom in the eyes? What am I supposed to tell her?

Concerned that other people might notice, I swallowed my tears and tried to console Kkeut-nyeo. "We thought we'd never get to go home, and here we are! We can worry about the future later. We've missed home so badly, and now we're nearly there!"

It wasn't Kkeut-nyeo as much as myself that I was trying to comfort. Mi-sun and Sam-rye's eyes were red from crying. I felt stifled down there in the cabin, so I squeezed my way through the crowd and went out to the deck. The vast ocean spread out all around me. The blue waves of the ocean rolled on with seeming indifference to what we'd endured.

I reminded myself of all the people who'd been buried so far from home like Bok-sun. I thought of the poor women who'd died in the air raid shelter. I thought of all the Koreans who'd drowned at sea while sailing to the front or back home and all the Koreans who'd been butchered on the battlefield. I should be thankful, I told myself, that I was even returning alive.

At dawn the next morning, the scarlet ball of the sun gave me a chill. The sun had the ghastly color of blood. Beautiful scenery didn't look very beautiful to me because of the wounds I'd suffered.

There was a cry from the people on deck.

"That's Oryukdo Island over there! It's Busan, Busan at last!"

"Hey, you're right! I can really see the island! And there's Busan, right next to it."

Everyone went back to their cabins to pack their luggage. I didn't have anything to pack.

We reached Busan Harbor a day and a half after setting out from Shimonoseki. The voyage had apparently taken half a day longer than expected because of mines in the water. A rumor was going around that a ship full of returnees had run into a mine and been blown up.

The ship was close to the shore now. Before it even reached the dock, the passengers all lined up, eager to set foot on Korean soil at once. But once the ship was tied up at the dock, we weren't allowed to disembark right away. First, we had to be checked for infectious diseases. When we were finally let off the ship the next day, we were sprinkled with white powder, which they called DDT. The song "Ship of the Returnees" was being played on the dock. The people listening wept and hugged each other.

Our guide gave us train tickets that would take us from Busan Station to our hometowns. Kkeut-nyeo had a ticket to Okcheon Station, while Sam-rye, Mi-sun, and I would continue on to Cheonan to transfer to other railway lines. From there, Sam-rye would take the Honam Line, while Mi-sun and I would get on the Janghang Line. When we boarded the train, it was so crammed with passengers we could barely move.

The whistle blew, and the train rolled through the countryside I'd dreamed of for so long. The fields were golden with the ripening ears of rice. It would soon be time for Kkeut-nyeo to get off at Okcheon Station. The other women and I each gave her a big hug and said our goodbyes.

"I want you to be happy and have a good life. Forget about everything that happened," Mi-sun said earnestly.

Kkeut-nyeo nodded, with tears in her eyes.

"You better get going. Have a good life—we all deserve that much!

"The same goes for you all. I want you to have a good life, too. Be happy and put the past behind you."

Even after saying goodbye, Kkeut-nyeo seemed reluctant to go. When the train blew its whistle, about to leave, she hurriedly stepped down.

The other two women and I got off the train at Cheonan. Sam-rye was supposed to transfer to the Honam Line, but she just stood there, sniffling and sobbing.

"What's the matter?" I said. "You need to hurry or you'll miss your train."

But Sam-rye shook her head. "The closer I get, the more scared I am of going home, Chun-ja. I'd rather not go back. I can't face my mom like this, let alone the rest of my family. I'm not going. You two go on, or you'll be late."

"What are you talking about? If you don't go home, what are you going to do?"

"I'm not scared of anything now. I'll live alone and pursue my studies, as I've always wanted to do. I won't starve to death if it's just me. Don't worry about me. You two should really get going."

Sam-rye seemed to have already made up her mind. As she waved to us, she passed through the turnstiles. Mi-sun and I stared numbly at Sam-rye as she walked away.

I could definitely relate to how Sam-rye felt. I'd been torn by the contrary desires to live by myself and to be with my family. At last, though, I'd decided to live with my family, at least for the time being. I missed my mom and Chun-sik so much, and I couldn't go on without seeing them.

Feeling a mixture of emotions, Mi-sun and I boarded the train on the Janghang Line. We were both supposed to get off the train at Hapdeok Station. Mi-sun had been away from home for three years, and I'd been away for eight. I'd left home to make some money, and it was crazy to think I was returning empty-handed. We'd be reaching Hapdeok in two hours at the most.

I'd left home in the spring, when the green leaves were starting to bud, and now it was the middle of autumn, with cosmos blossoms lining the train tracks. The sky looked as clear and empty as it had always looked at that time of year. The low hills were still marching along cheerfully, and the water in the streams flowed by with the same pleasant murmur I remembered from the past. As I returned home, it seemed as if everything was the same except for me and that I alone had been cast off into the cruel world.

Mi-sun and I alighted from the train together at Hapdeok Station.

"I guess it's time for us to part ways. I hope you can forget about everything and live a happy life."

"I hope you can, too, Mi-sun."

We held each other's hands and looked each other in the

eyes. In a moment, they filled with tears.

"As much as we may miss each other," Mi-sun said, as she blew her nose, "I don't think we should see each other again."

I completely understood what Mi-sun was saying. I nodded as I wiped the tears from my eyes. Mi-sun headed for Yesan, and I boarded the bus bound for Seosan. Now I was just one hour away from the home I'd dreamed of for so long.

I can't imagine how much I hurt Mom by going off like that without a single word. What am I supposed to tell her? Should I say that every day was a living hell?

But I couldn't tell her the truth. I didn't want to make her miserable.

I wonder if Chun-sik got married. He was just a boy of eleven years old when I left, so I guess he's a young man now.

So many thoughts whirled around my head. I was sure that as soon as I saw my mom, all that longing would turn into tears and gush down like a waterfall.

I shouldn't cry too much. I have to hold it back. What happens if Mom figures everything out? I can't let that happen.

As the bus got closer to home, I told myself to stay calm. At last, downtown Seosan came into view.

Seosan! I'm almost there.

When I stepped off the bus, the sun was already low in

the west. The realization that I'd been away for eight years but couldn't afford to pick up a pound of meat for my mom made me cry again.

Maybe I should say I didn't get paid because of the war. That might explain why it took me so long to get home.

All my possessions fit into a single bundle—just some underwear, a comb, and a towel, which I'd gotten at the POW camp. I didn't have anything to give my mom.

I walked from the bus stop in the direction of Hakdoljae. The red glow of the sunset hung above the rolling hills. Where the road forked, the heavy ears of rice rustled in the evening breeze, which carried a smack of the sea all the way from Ganwoldo Island. Tears flowed down as I breathed in the scents that had haunted my dreams: the rice growing in the paddies, the wind whispering through the pine trees, and the soil of my home. I rubbed my tears away before someone could see me crying and stared out into the distance. In the dusk of the evening, I fancied that Mt. Dobisan was whispering words of comfort for all that I'd suffered on my long journey.

At last, I reached the top of the pass at Hakdoljae. The lofty pines seemed to be looking down at me with pity.

I hope I don't run into someone I know!

I quickly walked along while peering around me, as if I were a criminal on the run.

Under the cluster of thatched roofs on the hillside, smoke billowed up from chimneys as the evening meal was prepared. Smoke was rising from the chimney at my house, too. Mom! I pictured her kindling a fire on the hearth. I could vaguely see someone moving around the yard, too.

Is that Mom or Chun-sik?

I hid behind a boulder on the hill and waited for it to get dark.

Darkness fell at last, and one by one, oil lamps began to glow in the village. That was when I started moving again. With every step on the ground I'd longed to walk upon, my feet seemed to be kissing the ground. Hearing a dog barking in one house, I started walking even faster. Finally, I was outside the gate in front of my house. I could see the glow of a lamp and my mom's silhouette through the rice paper covering the windows. I pushed open the gate and ran into the yard.

"Mom!" I tried to say, but my voice caught in my throat.

"Mom, I'm home!"

The door of the house swung open.

"Who—who's there? Is that—is that Chun-ja?"

My mom ran out in her bare feet.

"Oh, Chun-ja! What happened to you? You're alive, the gods be praised! Hurry inside!"

As my mom sobbed, I collapsed into her arms while my

own tears rained down.

"For heaven's sake, where have you been all this time? I thought my baby girl was dead!"

I clung tightly to my mom as we entered the house. The first thing I did was kneel to the ground and bow before her.

"You were gone for so long, and you didn't even write a single letter! Oh, never mind. You've made it back alive, and that's what matters."

My mom and I just cried, barely able to speak.

"I'm sorry, Mom. You don't know how much I missed you. Where's Chun-sik?"

Between her sobs, my mom said, "Two years ago, Chun-sik was taken to the coal mines in Japan. I figured I must have done something terrible in a previous life for my two healthy children to be taken away so suddenly. As it happens, I finally got a letter from Chun-sik just a few days ago."

My mom stroked my hands and patted my face, checking carefully to see if I'd been hurt. "The main thing is you made it back in one piece," she muttered to herself, still crying. "I made so many trips to Buseoksa Temple on Mt. Dobisan to pray for your safe return that I got blisters on my feet. Buddha and the gods brought you back to me."

It felt good to be cradled in my mom's arms like a little

child and to feel the warmth of her body. I didn't dare close my eyes because of the nightmares I might have. The joy of our reunion kept us awake through the night without the slightest feeling of drowsiness.

Looking at my mom's hands, I could tell how hard a time she'd had with her husband dead, her daughter vanished, and her son off in Japan. Given everything my mom had gone through, I couldn't bring myself to reveal my own wounds. I couldn't let her know that her daughter's womanhood had been taken from her. I couldn't let her know that I'd never get pregnant again, that I'd never experience the joy of getting married and having children.

Early the next morning, my mom got ready to go out. It had been too dark to see much the previous evening, but now I noticed to my dismay that her figure was gaunt and her face lined with wrinkles.

"Are you going somewhere, Mom?"

"You need to get ready, too, and be quick about it. The first thing we've got to do is give thanks to the Buddha for saving your life. You've been kept alive by the grace of the Buddha, and that's for sure!"

My mom handed me some new clothes. "Change into these. I made them for you while I was waiting for your return."

The new clothes were a black skirt and an aquamarine

jacket.

After getting changed, I went out into the yard, where it was obvious that the house had fallen into disrepair in her children's absence. The thatched roof was lumpy and needed some extra straw. Tears in the paper windows had been patched haphazardly. There were furrows in the yard that looked like the wrinkles on my mom's face. The stone wall, which had always been kept in good order, had gaps that looked like missing teeth. The only thing that hadn't changed was my mother's hardworking attitude.

I followed my mom to Buseoksa Temple. I didn't want to see anybody, but when she begged me to go, I couldn't turn her down. When I was little, I'd gone hand in hand with my mom to that temple on Buddha's birthday every April. As we climbed the hill, we heard the occasional cry of birds.

"I went to the temple more often than you would believe," my mom said. "I prayed for you and Chun-sik to come home safely. We owe everything to the Buddha. I was so relieved to learn that Chun-sik is safe, too. Mr. Yun lost contact with his son and doesn't even know if he's still alive."

Mr. Yun's son was my friend Jin-gyu.

I hope Jin-gyu makes it home safely, too!

The baby-faced soldiers that I'd serviced at the comfort station flashed through my mind, but I shook my head and pushed away those painful memories.

When we arrived at the temple, a monk pressed his palms together in greeting. My mom and I went into the main hall and joined the service, where I could barely hold back my tears. As we chanted the sutras to the rhythm of a monk striking a wooden bell, I silently prayed that the spirits of Bok-sun and Liam would find peace and that Jin-gyu would return home.

Leaving the hall after the service, I looked out at the dark-blue waters of the Yellow Sea. The tide had come in and covered the black rocks at the bottom of Changgae Bay. Far across the ocean, my blood-stained youth was frothing with a fearsome rage.

Within a few days, the news that I was back after an absence of eight years had spread throughout Hakdoljae. The village matrons stopped by to share their concerns with my mom. I was well past the marrying age, they said, and it was high time for my mom to find me a husband.

My mom brought up the subject with everyone she ran into. "If you hear of a good match, can you set my daughter up? They say there's nothing that brings as much good karma as arranging a marriage."

"That's right! I heard that setting up three couples is enough to get you through the gates of paradise. We'll do everything we can to find a spouse for Chun-ja soon."

The very next day, we started getting visits from all the matchmakers in the village. Their frequent visits made me uncomfortable.

After a while, I finally had it out with my mom. "I don't want to get married, Mom. I want to live with you. I can't leave you all by yourself when Chun-sik hasn't even made it home yet. It hurts to see you trying to marry me off as soon as I get home. So please tell all those old matchmakers to give it a rest."

My mom seemed afraid that I would tarnish our family's reputation for chastity. Her behavior made me feel more and more uncomfortable at home, even though I'd wanted so badly to return. I found myself wanting to run off and live by myself as Sam-rye had done.

One night, when the full moon was shining brightly, I couldn't seem to get to sleep. So I slipped out of the house and splashed my face with cold water as I breathed in the night air. After a while, I noticed that my mom was standing nearby and watching me. I wasn't sure how long she'd been there.

"Mom!"

"Yeah, we need to have a chat tonight. Come inside."

Without saying a word, I followed her into the house. I was about to light the lamp when she stopped me.

"Don't bother," she said in a low voice. "I think we'll find it easier to talk in the dark. You should put your mind at ease. I'm just grateful to the gods that you made it home alive."

When I heard this, my tears fell like a torrent. "Mom, I'm sorry."

"You didn't do anything wrong. It's all the fault of this wicked world. What can we do, aside from going on with our lives? You can tell me anything. Hiding the pain inside will just make it worse. You need to let go of those awful memories and make a new start. Oh, you poor thing!"

"I tried to kill myself."

"It's not your fault. It's the fault of those vile creatures who carried you off. I can't imagine how hard it all must have been for you, and at such a young age."

"Mom, I'm so sorry for coming back like this."

"You don't need to be sorry. Like I said, you're not to blame. Don't worry about me. I'm sure Chun-sik will be back soon. I guess living in such a tiny village makes things even worse."

My mom and I lay there together until early in the morning. After a while, she said, "Are you asleep?"

"No."

"If there's anything you want to say, get it off your chest."

"As you must have guessed, I can't get married. And so—" I said, and then bit my lip.

"But surely you don't have to grow old by yourself? And what will other people think?"

Mom let out a long sigh. I couldn't bring myself to tell her that my uterus had been removed.

"Maybe I could leave home for a while."

"I won't let you run off again now, when you just got back from the war! And we can't move until Chun-sik gets back, either."

There was nothing else I could say. I was finally home, but I was frustrated with myself for causing my mom so much pain.

I was afraid to be seen by the people in the village. I got nervous when someone paid us a visit or when I ran into someone while doing the laundry by the stream. I had the feeling that everyone was judging me and whispering about me behind my back.

The tightness in my chest got worse as the days went by. Sometimes, the only way to get relief was to pound on my chest with my fists. Sometimes, there seemed to be a fire burning inside, and gulping down cold water wouldn't cool the flames. My face would heat up until I could barely breathe and had to open the door to let some air in. I had trouble getting to sleep at night, too. I would bolt out of bed and rush outside to cool down.

Just sitting beside my mom was painful for me. This

wasn't the life I'd imagined when I'd come home, and I slowly started to hate other people.

That winter, Chun-sik returned from Japan, which at last brought me some relief. I made up my mind to ease my mom's burden by vanishing from the village.

Early one spring morning, the unmelted snow still glimmering on the peak of Mt. Dobisan, I slipped out of the house while my mom and Chun-sik were fast asleep. I didn't think it would be too hard to support myself. I had nothing to lose, and nothing more I could be robbed of.

I found that the best way to avoid people's notice was to live in the midst of them. I moved up to Seoul and did whatever work came to my hand. It was only by losing myself in my work that I could forget myself. It was only by forgetting myself—or rather, by pretending to forget—that I could manage, just barely, to cool the angry fire that blazed up inside of me from time to time. I tried to put out that fire by visiting one doctor after another and taking all kinds of supposed cures, but nothing helped. I couldn't even tell the doctors the truth of what had happened to me. I knew that the embers of anger inside me would never go out as long as I lived.

Three years after I came to Seoul, the Korean War broke out. I rushed back to my hometown to be with my mom. Chun-sik joined the army, and the villagers were distracted by the chaos of the war. And then while the war was winding down, and shortly before the armistice was signed, Chun-sik was killed in the Battle of White Horse, one of the bloodiest battles of the war.

I brought my mom to Seoul to live with me, where I took care of children who'd lost their parents in the war. Perhaps helping those children and watching them grow up satisfied the maternal instinct I could never act upon directly. Whenever my anger flared up again, the only way I could find peace was to devote my affection to those orphaned children. My mom stayed with me and helped with my work until she set out on that distant journey from which there's no return. My mom must have been heartbroken for me as a daughter until her dying day.

Around that time, I got married to a man in my neighborhood who'd lost his wife in an accident. I happened to find him in a moment of desperation and grief over his bereavement, when he was holding his baby girl in his arms, about to take his own life. It wasn't so much the man I wanted to save as his little girl. So I proposed to him and became his wife. I loved that girl more than anything in the world. My daughter brought healing to all my wounds and salvation to my cruelly violated soul.

But I wasn't always there for my husband. I wanted to give him my whole heart, but I felt too insecure to be the wife he needed me to be. In my heart, I wanted to love him, but I often struggled to act on those feelings. My husband wasn't satisfied with me, and so he sought love in other places. I couldn't bring myself to hate him for that. In fact, it would've been wrong for me to do so. I came to the full realization that perfect love can only be achieved when both body and mind are whole.

My daughter, the apple of my eye, grew into a lovely woman. She met a good man and got married. Then she gave birth to the little girl who would become dearer to me than anything else.

My granddaughter was a precious flower, even more precious than my own daughter. Watching her grow brought me supreme happiness. When she was out of my sight, I imagined all kinds of strange things. I was tormented by the fear that she'd be abducted and suffer the terrible things that I'd suffered. I couldn't bring those feelings under control.

In my anxiety, I sometimes crossed the line. Each time I acted impulsively, I regretted the results. I couldn't do anything about my obsession with my granddaughter. I would get agitated when I couldn't see her, despite knowing full well that I was hurting her and her mother. My rational mind warned me that I was going too far, but it was no use. The awful pain I'd suffered in the past slowly turned my obsession into a serious disease.

I was afraid of growing old. Every indication that I was losing the ability to control my body and mind made me tremble. I was frightened that my daughter and granddaughter might be affected by my past misfortune.

While I was watching TV one day, I saw a program about comfort women like me. The program was extremely painful to watch. I wanted to march right over there and demand that Japan apologize. That burning rage in my chest—which I'd thought had finally cooled—roared up again like lava. The way to cure my disease and find relief from the bitterness festering inside was to tell the world about the awful things I'd endured. But I was afraid that my precious daughter and granddaughter would learn the truth about me.

On the day my granddaughter graduated from elementary school, I decided to spend my final years at the House of Sharing. I left home without telling anybody. I had to make a break with my daughter and granddaughter in order to have the boldness to speak about my past and ask Japan for an apology.

In the end, the House of Sharing was a true resting place for me. It was painful to think how anxious my daughter must be, but I believed that time would bring her healing.

I'd been lucky enough to be given a daughter to raise and a granddaughter to love. What more could I want? Dozens of times every day, I feel the desire to go back to my daughter and granddaughter. But far stronger than that desire is my fear. I'm afraid that the people I love will be somehow tainted by the unhealed wounds inflicted by the Japanese soldiers who assaulted me.

I want my granddaughter to have a life that's happy and honorable. And so today, once again, I hide how much I miss her. Today, once again, while no one else is watching, I touch that tattered photograph and pray that she'll be able to enjoy a beautiful and happy life as a woman, the life I wasn't able to experience.

In this book, I've revealed all the horrible things I suffered as a comfort woman. I feel as if I've finally found peace. It was painful to dredge up the past to make this testimony, but it was all worth it in the end. Now I want to spend the rest of my life praying for all the people who died by my side in that terrible war.

Far from apologizing, Japan stubbornly refuses to admit the truth. I can never forgive Japan for its cruel murder of countless people and its merciless violations of human rights.

The truth of history will someday come to light. I believe that people have a sense of justice and a conscience and that those who defy them will never find peace. Today I'm still trying to forgive their poor souls, but the magma of rage is still seething inside me.

I hope that Japan will make a sincere apology so that our children can live in a peaceful world, a world where people are not exploited and abused, but treated with respect and dignity.

Keep the Statue Safe

Present day, Seoul

When Yu-ri finished reading her grandmother's oral history, she just sat there in silence for some time. It wasn't easy for her to accept that her grandmother had gone through such unimaginable horrors.

How could the Japanese have kidnapped a young girl and done such horrid things to her?

Chun-ja had suffered more than anyone could handle on their own.

It's hard to imagine how she endured such awful things by herself!

Yu-ri was convinced that her grandmother had made the right decision when she went to the House of Sharing.

I guess Mom knows the whole story, too. She must have been thunderstruck to learn that Grandma was her stepmom, and a comfort woman on top of that! I wonder who my real grandmother was.

There was no doubt that Yu-ri's maternal grandfather had been her mother's real father. Her mother had been an only child, and her grandfather had always said he'd fled North Korea during the Korean War and didn't have a single relative in South Korea. That meant there was no one Yu-ri could contact to ask about who her real grandmother might have been.

After reading the oral history book, Yu-ri finally understood why her grandmother had been so overprotective of her. Now all her bizarre behavior made sense.

I wonder how much Mom knows about Grandma's life.

After breakfast on Wednesday, a few days later, Yu-ri's mother was getting ready to go out.

Yu-ri decided it was time for the talk. "Are you going somewhere?"

"Hmm? Yeah, there's this thing I do on Wednesdays."

Yu-ri remembered what the director of the House of Sharing had told her. Intuitively, she knew her mother was headed to the Wednesday demonstration.

"Mom, I want to go with you. You're going to the Wednesday demonstration, right?"

This took Yu-ri's mother completely by surprise. "*You* want to go? To the Wednesday demonstration?"

"The thing is, I went to the House of Sharing last Saturday."

"The House of Sharing? You went by yourself?"

The staff at the House of Sharing had apparently kept Yu-ri's visit a secret, just as she'd asked.

"Yeah, I went by myself. And I brought back this book."

"What book is that? Oh, the oral history book came out! I've been looking forward to that. Did you read it already?"

After taking the book, Yu-ri's mother stared at it for a moment and then flipped it open to the section about Chun-ja.

"I'd been planning to tell you everything at some point," Yu-ri's mother said hesitantly.

"To be honest, Mom, I've been really upset with you lately. When I visited the House of Sharing, I was more interested in figuring out what was going on with you than with Grandma. But now that I've read the oral history book, I understand both of you."

"That's sweet of you, Yu-ri. Even now, I find it hard to believe. For my whole life, I had no idea of how much pain your grandmother was in. I'm disgusted with myself. I was such a selfish daughter. I'm ashamed to say that when everyone was talking about the comfort woman issue, I didn't think it had anything to do with me. I can't express how guilty I feel about your grandmother. Since I met those old women at the House of Sharing, I've felt guilty about them, too. The worst part is that it took me so long to care."

Yu-ri's mother pulled out a handkerchief and dabbed at the tears running down her cheeks.

"What if Grandma had told us the whole truth before she died?"

"The fact that she wasn't my real mother doesn't really matter. What really gets me is how uncaring a daughter I was. I really regret that. I was embarrassed to tell you what a pathetic daughter I was. I kept thinking I'd tell you everything one of these days, but I couldn't work up the courage."

Yu-ri's mother broke off and just stood there for a while, her shoulders heaving.

Yu-ri wanted to comfort her mother. "You're not the only one who feels like that. I was always getting irritated by Grandma, and I wasn't interested in the comfort women, either. I bet my friends are the same way. So you're not the only one!"

Yu-ri's mother slowly shook her head, her eyes bloodshot.

"I'm ashamed that it took your grandmother's death to bring me some self-awareness. I couldn't help it when I was little, I guess, but even now that you've grown up so much, I never gave much thought to what might be ailing your grandmother. If I'd had an ounce of maturity, I would've tried to figure out why my parents fought so much. Your grandmother did a lot of things that were just baffling, of course. But every time, I treated her like a weirdo. I would just gripe about how neurotic or eccentric she was. Not one time did I try to understand the feelings that might be behind her behavior. That's what I regret so much."

"Even if you'd asked her, she wouldn't have told you the truth."

"I'm not so sure about that. If I'd been a more loving daughter and if I'd taken interest in her and tried to help her deal with her issues, I might've been able to lighten her burden. The fact that I didn't do so is what's so distressing."

Yu-ri's mother was still shaking her head. "Your grandmother was so utterly devoted to me that our friends and family were concerned about how overprotective she was. Because of that, I was really self-centered growing up."

"Grandma wouldn't want you to be so hard on yourself, Mom."

"When I said I was done having kids after giving birth to you, your grandmother threw a real fit. Now I finally know why. The hardest thing for her must have been the fact that she couldn't have kids, because of the hysterectomy the Japanese gave her. Your grandmother gave me her love, but I never gave her anything in return. I also feel guilty about you, Yu-ri. I may seem a little distant for a while, until I manage to forgive myself. You'll understand, won't you?

"I wish you wouldn't beat yourself up so much, Mom. Grandma said that you and I brought her happiness. What I'm trying to say is—"

Yu-ri suddenly felt a lump in her throat. The fact was that she had plenty of regrets, too.

"Even so, it's a good thing that Grandma had a chance to tell her story in the oral history book before she passed away. From now on, I want to play a big role in helping her find peace."

"That's a good idea. The women at the House of Sharing are all old, and there's no telling how much longer they have. We really don't have much time left. We've got to get a decent apology out of Japan and protect the comfort women statue."

"All right! It's time that I got involved, for Grandma's sake. Let me go with you to the Wednesday demonstration."

Yu-ri's mother wrapped her arms around her shoulders. Only a few weeks had passed since Yu-ri's middle school graduation, but so much had happened since then that it felt more like months. It seemed to Yu-ri that her relationship with her mother was finally back on track.

Yu-ri thought about how her grandmother had left a record of her terrible story—being robbed of years of her life, as well as her uterus. That record was a page of Korea's tragic history. Lunatics who thought nothing of human life had dared to play God. They'd had the temerity to pluck flowers before they could bloom, violating the female organs that are made to shelter the sacred seeds of life. Those were terrible, unforgiveable crimes.

Yu-ri searched online to see if there was anything else aside from the Wednesday demonstration that she could do before high school started in a few days. She read about some female university students who were camped out across from the Japanese embassy by the statue of a young girl that represented the comfort women. The student protesters stayed up all night in front of the embassy, even when the weather was cold and snowy, to make sure that no one removed the statue. If those protesters were sacrificing so much for the comfort women, Yu-ri thought, she ought to be even more committed. After all, she was the granddaughter of a comfort woman!

Yu-ri's heart raced with excitement at having found something she could do for the comfort women. As soon as her tutoring session was over, she headed to the Japanese embassy. The protesters were still there, keeping watch over the comfort woman statue in a makeshift shelter of plastic sheeting. Yu-ri arranged to spend the next night at the shelter and then went home.

The next evening, Yu-ri donned some heavy-duty winter

clothing and grabbed a knit cap and fur-lined boots.

"Mom, I've found something I can do for Grandma," Yu-ri announced.

Her mother looked at her outfit in bewilderment.

"Where are you off to at such a late hour?"

"I made plans with the student protesters. I'm going to keep watch over the comfort woman statue."

"There's a nasty wind blowing now right because of the cold front. It's freezing out there!"

"No matter how cold it gets, it's nothing compared to what Grandma went through. Go on to bed, Mom, and don't worry about me."

"I saw on TV how those students are camped out by the statue to make sure no one bothers it," Yu-ri's mother said as she handed Yu-ri a couple of hand warmers. "Well, go ahead then. But give me a call if you get too cold. I'll be there to pick you up right away."

Yu-ri gulped hard as tears stung her eyes. "I'm a high school student now. I'm not a little kid! I'll come back if I can't hack it."

Yu-ri saw tears gleaming in her mother's eyes. She stuffed the hand warmers into a backpack along with a blanket and then set off at a brisk pace.

A cold wind raked Yu-ri's cheeks, and snowflakes blew through the air. The women who'd promised to meet Yu-ri that evening were already in the shelter. Yu-ri sat down beside them.

Yu-ri and the other protesters laid a mat on the ground, but that didn't keep the cold away. Passersby handed them some more hand warmers.

Yu-ri looked at the slogans the protesters had written on their signs. One said, "Scrap the deal with Japan!"

If only Grandma could've gotten a real apology from the Japanese government before she died!

Sitting there, Yu-ri couldn't stop shivering. But she stayed strong, reminding herself that this was nothing compared to what her grandmother had lived through. Yu-ri also had the other protesters to keep her spirits up. They blew on each other's hands and wrapped blankets around each other's feet. The pedestrians gradually thinned out, and the sounds of the demonstration died down.

"You've got to stay awake out here. It's dangerous to fall asleep in the cold. If you get drowsy, try pressing on your fingertips. Poking the soles of your feet can also keep you awake."

One of the other protesters was giving Yu-ri some tips when someone walked up holding a big bundle. It was Yu-ri's mother.

"Hey, Yu-ri! Are you doing all right?"

"Mom? Why are you here?"

"I'm afraid I got a tongue lashing from your grandmother. She wasn't happy I sent you out here on such a cold night. So here I am. I brought a comforter, too. You don't mind me joining you, do you?"

The other protesters gaped at Yu-ri and her mother in confusion.

"Everyone, this is my mom."

After they'd all exchanged greetings, Yu-ri's mother crawled through the plastic sheets and took a seat.

Now that I think about it, I guess I would've made an appearance, too, if I were Mom. She's Grandma's daughter, after all!

Patting the foot of the comfort woman statue, Yu-ri whispered to herself.

Grandma! Mom and I are going to make the world a better place, just like you wanted. And we'll keep the statue safe, too!

A Message from the Author

Though Koreans suffered many things during Japan's colonial occupation of the peninsula, it would be impossible to overemphasize the horrors endured by the "comfort women," the euphemism used to refer to the women conscripted to be sex slaves for the Japanese army.

Negotiations between the foreign ministers of South Korea and Japan and a phone call between the two countries' leaders culminated in an agreement, signed on December 28, 2015, that the two governments declared was a permanent solution to the comfort woman issue. Unfortunately, though, that agreement didn't satisfy everyone.

The story of the comfort women has been on my mind for a long time, but I hesitated to write about it. The terrible things those women suffered weren't easy to put into words. Many people have a general understanding of their suffering, but I wanted this book to be a comprehensive treatment of the subject. I strove to include accurate depictions of horrors that hadn't appeared in previous books. Countless times during the composition of this book, I would have to pause for a while to bring my emotions under control before I could resume writing.

I made up my mind to write this book after reading an article about Japanese photojournalist Takashi Ito. In a book of photographs taken on two visits to North Korea in 1999 and 2015, Ito made the following remarks:

"While staying in Pyongyang for nineteen days in May and June of this year, I interviewed many victims. I was particularly shocked by the testimony of the former comfort women, or sex slaves for the Japanese army, and by the deep scars on their bodies."

After Ito saw how Korean comfort women had been horribly injured by Japanese soldiers—his own countrymen—during the Pacific War, he published a book that contained candid photographs of those women and detailed accounts of their experiences. I was staggered and horrified to read in the article that some of the comfort women had had to undergo hysterectomies.

Ito thoroughly uncovered and recorded the unforgivable sins committed by the Japanese soldiers. Not only had they taken these young women and used them as tools for satisfying their sexual desires, but when their defeat was imminent, they buried countless people alive in their retreat. I was greatly encouraged by the fact that it was a Japanese reporter who revealed to the world the inhumane, impious, and barbaric behavior of the Japanese army. This stood in sharp contrast to the Japanese government, which to this day has never made a genuine apology and continues to deny and conceal most of what happened.

This book is the latest of several historical novels I've written about Japan's colonization of Korea, and like my earlier novels, it's grounded in the facts of history.

Many of my books touch on how Koreans have suffered at the hands of the Japanese. *The Dark Sea* is about a horrible accident at the Chosei coal mine. Young Koreans who'd been press-ganged by the Japanese to work in slave-like conditions died when the mine collapsed, and their bodies remain there to this day. *The Children of Henequen* is the sad story of starving people who were betrayed by Japan and sold to Mexico. *The Kareiski's Endless Wandering* is the story of Koreans living in Russia and Primorsky Krai who were forcibly removed to Central Asia by Stalin because of fears that they might become spies for Japan. *Choe Jae-hyeong: Independence Fighter* is about the financial backer of freedom fighters such as Ahn Jung-geun in Primorsky Krai, which was the initial center of Korea's independence movement. *Hagi: Lady of the Court* deals with the tragic fate of Empress Myeongseong, who was cruelly murdered by the Japanese.

As a woman, the hardest challenge I've faced in any

of these books was depicting the horrible things that the comfort women endured. But I derived great courage from what I felt was my mission: presenting the unhappy facts of history without any embellishments or omissions.

As sorry as I feel about digging up the painful past of the comfort women, that past is something we're obliged to learn. I wanted to denounce the Japanese army for its awful atrocities, if only to ensure that this tragic history is never repeated.

The sad fact is that the surviving comfort women are passing away, one by one. I pray that those who are still with us may enjoy good health. As for the departed, my prayer is that, in the next life, they will get to pursue the dreams that were crushed while they were still young girls, before they had a chance to bloom.

Moon Young-sook
Liberation Day, August 15, 2016

Moon Young-sook

Moon Young-sook was born in Seosan, Chungcheongnam-do, in 1953. Her literary career took off when she won the second Blue Literature Prize in 2004 and the sixth Literature Neighborhood Prize for Children's Literature in 2005. In 2012, she received a creative grant from the Seoul Foundation for Arts and Culture.

Moon mostly writes stories to teach young people about parts of Korean history that Koreans must never forget. Some of her best-known works are the young adult historical novels *The Kareiski's Endless Wandering* and *The Children of Henequen*. She has also written children's novels including *Picture in the Tomb, The Dark Sea, Hagi: Lady of the Court, The Coat of Many Colors, The Old Man Who Became a Baby,* and *The Bread of Kaesong.*

Translator   David M. Carruth

After graduating from John Brown University in Arkansas with a bachelor's in English literature in 2006, David Carruth moved to South Korea. During eight years as a full-time Korean-English translator, he has worked extensively with both fiction and nonfiction. He has translated a number of books, including *Across the Tumen*, another historical novel for young adults by Moon Young-sook.

Credits

Publisher	Kim Hyunggeun
Translator	David M. Carruth
Editor	Kim Daniel
Copy Editor	Anna Bloom
Proofreader	Lee Kyehyun
Designer	Lee Chan-mi
Cover Illustrator	Kim Min-kyung